THE PERFECT PLAY

BRITNEY M. MILLS

CRYSTAL CANYON PRESS

CHAPTER 1

PENNY

Today could determine my future, and, of course, I was running late. My junior year softball tryouts were starting in a few hours and, while I'd never worried about making the cut even as a freshman, we had a new coach this year. I knew I was ready to take over as the ace pitcher for the Rosemont Royals softball team after Sara Dempsey graduated last year, but who knew what would happen when I'd only met Coach Ambrose a couple of times at open-gym practices? I needed to earn a scholarship, and I needed it bad.

Mornings were never my favorite, but in the last week, I was dragging my body out of bed when my alarm went off. Between my hours waitressing at the diner, schoolwork, and practicing pitches out in the backyard with every spare minute left over, it seemed there was never enough time in the day for all I needed to get done.

After a quick shower and change, I made my way to the kitchen, hoping my little brother hadn't eaten the rest of my favorite sugary cereal.

"Good morning, sunshine," my dad said over his morning

cup of coffee. His eyes darted back to the newspaper before him, and I didn't even have to look to see what he was studying. The classifieds.

My father had been looking for new work since my mother left before my eighth-grade year, hoping to either add to the small cash flow he already had or find something better that he qualified for. He'd worked for a local landscaper for nearly eight years, and I knew he wished he could afford to send me to college after I graduated next year, but it just wasn't realistic. At this point, I knew a full-ride scholarship was the only way I would make it through college debt-free. And with my end goal being to become a family therapist, every little bit helped.

"Morning, Dad." I pulled a bowl from a cabinet and opened another one where the cereal was usually stored. A red box appeared in my peripheral vision, and I picked it up, feeling only the weight of the cardboard box. Derrick had already beaten me to it. I gritted my teeth, trying to curb the anger fizzing in my stomach. "Why couldn't he just let me have it this one time?"

"What?" My dad looked up, trying to figure it out. "Oh, uh, your cereal. Yeah, Derrick said something about you being mad at him. I think he's gone to hide in his room until you leave. It's probably good that eighth grade starts later than the high school." The corners of his mouth turned up, the mischief in his eyes only driving my anger up this morning.

I held the box up, wishing I could start this morning over already. Maybe if I'd gotten up the first time my alarm sounded, I would be delighting in my favorite cereal before a big day of tryouts.

I couldn't help but feel my future depended on this season. Not that I expected to get recruited from my high school team. My summer ball competition team was the key when it came to that, but high school softball was more about pride for me. My mom had played at Rosemont High years ago, and even though she was gone and I didn't want to care about her opinion of me, this was where I felt it the most. I wanted to break her records and have my number retired. To see my jersey hanging in the school trophy box, just so that if she ever did decide to come back and see what her kids had been up to since she'd taken off, she could feel both ashamed and proud.

Shaking off those thoughts, I pulled the box of dried cardboard flakes from the cupboard and filled my bowl, adding plenty of milk and a scoop or two of sugar. Okay, more like five scoops. I couldn't choke those down without at least some flavor to enjoy.

I slumped into the seat across from my father, dunking my cereal several times in the milk.

"Tryouts today?" My dad wasn't known for overusing words.

"Yeah, right after school. We have that new coach this year, Coach Ambrose. I just hope I make the cut." At my words, my insides turned a bit.

Folding up the paper, he said, "You'll be just fine, Penny Davis. The Royals wouldn't have made it to fifth in state last year without you. Just go out there and show this new coach what you've got." He gave me a reassuring smile, just as he did every time things seemed a little hard. Like when my mother left.

"Have you thought any more about starting your own company, Dad?" I asked, scooping the flakes into my mouth. It was a conversation we'd had several times over the last year, and I still thought it would be better for him to start his own company than labor for his boss for the next twenty years, who took more trips throughout the year than actually working. My dad had thought about it more and more as the year went on, but he hadn't made the jump yet.

He shook his head, his sad smile conveying more than words could right now. Starting a lawn care company had a lot of upfront costs, namely the ride-on mowers and buying a trailer to haul it all. Then there was the fact that he'd have to buy a truck that would be able to handle pulling the equipment around town.

"I have to cut the lawn over at the Donovan place and then I'll be at the Montgomerys' the rest of the day." He stood, taking his coffee mug with him and rinsing it in the sink. "If I'm not home when you get back, will you start dinner? You know how big their lawn is, and I might be there until late."

The Montgomerys could have fit several softball fields on their property, so cutting and maintaining it usually took hours. But from what my dad said, they were generous about tipping him. We didn't necessarily live in a bad neighborhood, but it was about as middle class as we could get.

"I'm scheduled at the diner for tonight. Is there something easy Derrick could make?" I tipped the bowl so I could drink the last of the milk and then moved to join him at the sink.

"We probably have a few boxed meals left in the pantry. I'll set some meat out so it'll be ready for him. But it might be a good idea to ask Sherri to watch out for flames while we're both gone." He chuckled, drying his hands on a towel before passing it to me.

The Whites had been our next-door neighbors since before I could remember. Sherri was a kind woman, but there was always a sadness to her, probably due to her husband always traveling for work. She had twin daughters a year younger than Derrick, as well as a son my age, Jake. The cockiest, most stubborn kid I'd ever met in my life.

Jake hadn't always been that way, and there were times I

longed for those days when we could tell each other about anything, usually while tossing a ball back and forth. The random flashes of earlier times just dredged up all the betrayal I felt at him ditching me three and a half years ago. Like he was too cool to hang out with a nerdy tomboy, especially now that he was Mr. Popular at Rosemont High.

I scrubbed the dish with more force than I should have, only realizing it when the bristles of the brush scraped my fingers. Setting the bowl in the dish drainer, I said goodbye to my dad and headed out to my ancient Honda Civic, closing my eyes in the hopes that it would start up just one more time for me. I'd tried jiggling the key in the ignition once a few weeks ago when it wouldn't start, and it had become a sort of ritual.

The engine roared to life, and I breathed a sigh of relief, easing out of the driveway and onto the road. School was nearly four miles to the south, but there were several intersections with long lights on the route, meaning I was cutting it close. I noticed Jake's forest-green Jeep still in his driveway and rolled my eyes. Of course, he hadn't left yet.

Once I made it to school and parked, I hurried into the common area. Spotting two of my good friends, Kate and Serena, I grinned and waved as I walked over to them.

"Hey, cutting it a little close today, aren't you, Pen?" Kate asked, looking down at her phone. A few seconds later, the first bell rang.

"I couldn't drag myself out of bed this morning," I said, waiting for them to stand so we could walk down the hall together. We all had the same first period, which made it fun for me. Other than that, I didn't have any classes with any of the other girls in our friend group. They were always talking about what happened in their joint classes, and I was just trying to hide the fact that I'd had to read sixty of the most snooze-worthy pages of history the night before for my advanced class.

Kate grinned. "Well, if you didn't have the hardest schedule this school offers, you might get a little more sleep, or at least some time to hang out with your friends." She jabbed her elbow into my side, reminding me once again just how much taller I was. Just two inches shy of a whole foot difference, I usually felt like a giant unless Brynn was around.

We walked into class and took our seats at the back of the room, ready for choir to begin. Why they had choir so early in the morning, I'll never understand. My voice never sounded normal until closer to lunch.

"Do you want to go grab food with us after the game tonight?" Serena asked. The girls basketball team had made it to the semi-finals, and Brynn was the starting center. Kate had to go to the game as one of the student body officers for Rosemont High, and Serena just loved any excuse to get out of the house since the volleyball season had wrapped up.

"Raincheck? I have tryouts after school, and then I have to work at the diner."

Kate frowned. "Good luck today. We should do something this weekend when you're free. Or are you working all weekend too?"

"That would be fun. I get next week's schedule tonight, so I'll let you know." It wasn't the first time I'd gotten the third degree from my friends. The only other one of us with a job was Hazel, but her hours were more flexible. My job was necessary to just survive. My father barely made enough to allow us to keep living in the home we had, which meant any school fees, softball fees, gas and insurance, or minor expenses that came up were my responsibility.

There were times when I wished my life could be as simple as theirs, as simple as it was when my mother was living with us, her job making her the breadwinner. But those feelings usually fled as soon as I remembered what she'd done to us.

The pit in my stomach formed, and I bit the corner of my lip harder than I should have. We were doing just fine without her, and it wasn't possible to put a price on the peace that came with minimal fighting in the house.

I went through my success checklist for the future, hoping it would help ease the anxiety pulling me in different directions:

1. Pass my AP tests in four months.

2. Get seen by college coaches this summer.

3. Get a scholarship.

4. Help kids of divorced parents as a family therapist.

I felt better. Having something in my control to cling to made a world of difference. I could study enough to pass those classes. I could practice enough to impress college coaches. And I was willing to put in the time to become the best therapist there was. The only thing out of my control was the scholarship, but if I gave it my all, then something was sure to come through. At least, that's what I continued to tell myself.

Mrs. Dublin began class with our usual warm-up routine, and I tried to focus on the sounds, hoping it would ease my anxiety about tryouts later. I'd never worried like this with the last coach we'd had, but Coach Ambrose's reputation as the softball coach at Pecan Flatts, one of our rival high schools, was that she was strict and tough on her players. I could handle all that, but if she played favorites and Tammy Starling got to pitch over me, I could kiss broken records and my jersey hanging in the trophy case goodbye.

Everything would work out. It had to.

CHAPTER 2

*P*ulling into the parking lot of the school as the last bell rang, my brain worked to map out the shortest route to my first-period class. Hopefully, I wouldn't get caught by an administrator. I already had enough tardies to last until the end of time, and while I knew I was going to have to work them off at some point, it didn't motivate me to get to class on time.

Walking through the locker-room door, I checked both directions before darting out far enough to swing around the handrail and onto the stairs to my history class upstairs. Maybe luck was working in my favor today because I moved into the classroom when Ms. Lovell had her back turned. There were a few snickers, but I tried to keep my face neutral, hoping she wouldn't notice I'd just shown up.

"Will someone please tell me the difference between the Baroque and the Victorian eras?" Ms. Lovell asked, turning around to face the class.

"If it ain't Baroque, don't fix it," I mumbled.

The students around me who'd heard it chuckled along as the teacher's eyes narrowed in on me. Her lips formed a tight line, and she looked as though I'd already started pushing buttons I shouldn't have. "Thank you, Mr. White, for actually joining us at a more normal time. Would you like to repeat what you just said?"

I raised a hand, slouching into my seat even more. "I'm good."

Her laser eyes seemed to bore into me for another few seconds before moving to the hand raised on the other side of the room. "Yes, Kara."

I shook my head, wishing I could be back in my comfortable king-sized bed, dreaming about anything but being here. Only a few more hours until baseball, which I could handle. It was the only thing keeping me sane these days, and I couldn't wait for a little batting practice. There was nothing better than feeling the ball connect with the bat just right and go sailing over the fence.

Class ended soon enough, and then lunch passed with little fanfare. A few of the guys and I grabbed some drive-thru food at one of the local restaurants and ate it on the way back to the school.

Dax Stratton had driven, and I was riding up front, with Ben, Nate, and Colt in back. "What do you think Coach Maddox will have us do today?" Dax asked, turning down the radio a few notches.

"Probably make us run 'til we puke. Isn't that what we had to do last year for tryouts?" Ben Clark was our ace pitcher and one of the reasons we'd made it so far in the state tournament the year before.

"Don't say that," I said between bites of my bacon cheeseburger. "I don't need to taste all this coming back up." I pointed to the food in my hand, and the guys chuckled.

Nate Everton, a sophomore and the youngest of the group, patted his stomach. "This iron stomach can handle whatever Coach deals us today."

"Iron stomach? Didn't you just throw up at that party a couple of weeks ago?" I teased, turning my head back to see his reaction.

"I spit out the weird fishy appetizer. I did not throw up. There's a difference, man." Nate's eyebrows stitched together, and he looked like he was reliving the experience.

Colt Buttars sat next to one of the back windows. "Let's just hope we don't have to stay longer than the softball team again. How do they always get out so early?"

Every time softball came up, my mind automatically went to Penny Davis, my next-door neighbor. The girl was always out practicing in her backyard, the *thunk, thunk, thunk* of the ball hitting off the mat on the shed she pitched against in her backyard. I'd watched her a few days ago from my window, surprised at how accurate her pitches had gotten over the past few years, slipping through the small target holes her father had cut into the rubber mat. She still signaled when her change-up was coming, though. At least I could still pick up on that.

I'd played shortstop for years, but back in the day, I was the one she pitched to, and I'd given her pointers here and there. A lot had changed in a few years, and I couldn't remember the last time I'd spoken to her.

"Jake? Are you in there, man?" Dax was waving his hand across my face, and I shook my head, pulling myself out of long-forgotten memories. Of a simpler time when I didn't wake up with nightmares of the accident.

I pushed Dax's long arm away and opened the passenger door. "I'm fine. Just hoping we can do more batting practice than running today."

Ben snickered. "That won't happen. Not on the first day at least. That's how Coach weeds them out from the beginning, remember?" There were always plenty of kids at tryouts, ones who hadn't practiced since their machine-pitch youth and had decided they were suddenly going to join the team without practicing beforehand. Coach Maddox liked to make things difficult the first day to see who would show up for day two.

We walked back to the school, and I groaned. Chemistry was my last class of the day and my least favorite of all time. Why couldn't science be just about the experiments instead of balancing equations?

"I'm this way," I said, pointing down the other hall. The guys waved and continued chatting as they moved away. I took a few steps and turned, bumping into someone. Papers and notebooks flew in several directions, looking like a giant snowstorm around us.

"Watch where you're going, jerk." The voice was familiar, and seeing the auburn hair pulled back in what looked like a bird's nest of a ponytail told me it was the girl I'd thought about minutes before.

Standing there, I debated whether or not to help her pick up the mess around us. "Nice to see you too, Nickel."

Penny's head flicked up to glare at me, her lips pinched together in a way that gave me satisfaction from using the old nickname she'd always hated.

"You can at least help me pick some of this up, you know. I'm going to be late this period." She was busy scooping papers together, and I finally bent down and picked up the notebook. The front was covered in scribbles.

"'I heart question mark,'" I read aloud. Giving her a half-smile, I said, "Oh, does Nickel have a secret crush? And instead of writing initials, she's being exceptionally vague."

She snatched the notebook from my hands and gathered everything, standing quickly. With a lick of her lips that drew my eyes, she brushed a loose piece of hair out of her face. "That's none of your business, and it hasn't been for a long time. I'm surprised you even remember who I am."

The comment stung a bit, but I had to keep my expression neutral. I wasn't about to show weakness, not even when we'd shared so much in the past. And not that we'd ever discussed our crushes back when we were friends, but the thought intrigued me. Who would this tom-boy be into?

She walked down the hall, her legs stretching out longer and longer until she was practically speed walking.

"What? Don't want to talk to your old friend Jake?"

"Not particularly, no." Her eyebrows scrunched together, and her face puckered like she'd swallowed something bitter. I tried to think of the last time I'd seen her smile. Probably a few days ago when she was walking through the hall with her friends. But the last time she'd directed one at me? Years, probably. But it wasn't like that should bother me.

We walked a few more paces in silence as I tried to think of something that would annoy her more. "I heard you guys got a new coach. How do you think he'll be?"

"It's a woman. And what's with all the interest in softball all of a sudden?" She stopped and turned to look at me. Her gaze sent an odd sensation through my body, making me feel like I didn't have control of the situation. I didn't like it when I didn't have control.

I shrugged, trying to push the feeling away. Raising my hands in surrender, I said, "I just thought I'd ask. We're still neighbors, and I thought I'd try to chat for a minute. But it seems we're going to be late, and I know how you are about being on time." I turned and continued down the hall, hearing her footsteps scuttle behind me.

I walked into my classroom and heard her say, "Good luck on your tryouts today," before heading into the classroom next door. One of the advanced-placement classes. I had no idea she was even taking one of those. For a moment, I felt guilty that someone with whom I'd been so close growing up was now practically a stranger.

The phrase on the front of her notebook had me even more curious. I'd have to find out who it was just so I could know who Penny Davis had a crush on. It would give me something to think about as my chemistry teacher droned on.

13

CHAPTER 3

PENNY

*M*y cheeks still felt hot long after bumping into Jake Davis. What a jerk. I'd gone through withdrawals of talking to him after he stopped hanging out with me three and a half years before, but it had been a long time since I'd even thought about him besides the occasional sighting in the halls or him getting into his Jeep next door. We'd been able to tell each other just about anything, until he shut me out.

I traced my fingers over the letters on my notebook, the ones Jake had read out loud. Of all the people to see that, why did it have to be him? I'd had this notebook for the last year and a half. Crazy, I know, but I wrote so small that a semester's worth of classes only filled up about half the pages in each section.

My mind went back to when I'd written them at the very beginning of sophomore year, when I'd had a crush on two guys. I didn't want people to put together initials, so I'd written the question mark. Since Johnny Goodman had moved away halfway through last year, I hadn't really thought about what I'd written, just doing everything I could to pass my honors classes. When Jake read it earlier, I wanted to crawl into a hole.

I'd always liked Jake, always had a small crush on him, even when we were best friends. And I wished I could be rid of him now, that seeing him every once in a while didn't cause something in me to jump or my pulse to race. But it was still there, and no matter how hard I tried to tell myself I didn't like him, there was still a small bit of doubt holding its ground like the captain on a battlefield.

But there was absolutely no chance there. Jake was Rosemont royalty as he swaggered through the hallways, and I—well, I was a nerdy athlete, which meant my social status at school was near the bottom.

Not to mention that since the accident, it seemed as though the Jake I'd grown up with had been completely kidnapped, leaving a newer, stranger version in his place. I sometimes wondered what life would have been like had we never drifted apart. But would that mean I'd be in as much trouble as Jake or, worse, dead like Troy Johnson?

It couldn't have been all Jake's fault. He wasn't driving, but he didn't do anything to keep Troy from getting behind the wheel. At least, from what I heard.

History class passed much faster than normal, and soon enough I was in the girls' locker room, changing into my shorts and long socks for tryouts. It was the end of January in Texas, so I grabbed my sweatshirt in case I needed it. I redid my ponytail, hoping it would stay in for the rest of the day. I wouldn't have time to keep retying my waist-length hair, and I didn't want to do anything to be on the new coach's bad side.

"What do you think we'll have to do for tryouts?" a bunch of the other excited girls asked.

I gave them a nod and a small smile. With butterflies in my stomach, I was ready, even for the lengthy amounts of running most coaches liked to introduce on the first day. I'd been waiting all day—no, all month—for this. Because once Christmas was over, this had been the next best-anticipated event, and I just needed to make it through.

I grabbed my bat bag and moved out the back doors to the softball field. It took a few minutes to walk there, but at least it was on our school campus, which wasn't true of every high school. Our outfield fence was only about twenty yards from the guys' fence, but we were on the far side, having to walk down the long gravel road to get there.

I laced up my cleats and did a few stretches, hoping to get rid of some of the excitement and anxiety bubbling inside me.

"Here goes another season," a familiar voice said behind me.

I turned and grinned at Jessie, my catcher. We'd been together since we started competition softball at the age of eleven, and I trusted her with my life.

"Yep. It feels like we just finished up last season, and here we are again."

Jessie pulled her glove out of her bag and stood, tossing the ball into it over and over again. "Yeah, but this year we're upperclassmen. No more lugging gear forever."

I couldn't agree more. That was the hardest thing about being one of the freshmen or sophomores on the team. We were two of three sophomores the year before, with only two other freshmen, meaning we still had a lot of the responsibility of water bottles, the bag of bats, and the endless buckets of balls our previous coach required each practice.

I grabbed my glove from my bag and jogged backward a few paces. Jessie tossed the ball and I caught it, the snapping sound from my glove calming some of my anxiety. I knew how to do this, and no matter what the new coach would be like, I just had to keep focused and give it my all.

"What's he doing over there?" Jessie asked as she threw the ball again.

I waited to catch it before turning in the direction she was looking. I didn't look long as I saw Jake White with his forearms resting on top of the fence, looking in our direction. I turned my back to him and threw the ball back with more force than I'd intended.

"Whoa, Pen. What was that?" Jessie had barely caught the ball before it hit her face, and I knew I was going to get it.

Shaking my head, I said, "Sorry. I ran into him before last period today, and I'd be lying if I said I don't want to strangle him sometimes."

"Weren't you two really good friends at one point? I remember him coming to a bunch of our games when we were twelve and thirteen."

Sour bile crept into my throat, and I swallowed it down. "Yeah, but that was a lifetime ago. I'm not cool enough for his group anymore."

I took several steps backward to lengthen the throws before moving back in to warm up throwing underhand. It was our routine to get to the field early and work on pitches as the rest of the team trickled in. It allowed me the maximum time to work on each pitch, making sure I was improving since I had to work after practice.

"I didn't expect to see anyone out here so early," said the coach as she walked over with a few bags slung over her shoulder. "Penny and Jessie, right?"

Jessie nodded, and I smiled at her, spinning the ball in my right hand a few times. A surge of anxiety hit my stomach, and I gripped the ball before winding up and letting go. The ball missed the strike zone by several inches, but I'd gotten some speed on it, causing a loud snap to come from Jessie's glove and helping the tension release a bit.

"Looks good," Coach Ambrose said. She set her stuff down and walked over to me. "What pitches do you throw?"

I licked my lips as I decided on my response. "The riseball is my favorite. I've got a good curve, and my change-up throws a lot of people off. I've been working on a screwball and a drop, but those aren't as effective."

She nodded, sticking her hands in her windbreaker pants pockets. "Okay, show me what you've got, Davis."

I threw a few of the different pitches and focused on the mound each time I got the ball back from Jessie.

Coach Ambrose finally nodded. "It looks really good. And after all the information I researched on you, we just might have a state title this year for Rosemont." She grinned at me. "Of course, you still have to make it through today's tryouts."

She walked away, and Jessie shrugged her shoulders, as confused as I was. She'd researched my stats? Why did that surprise me? It was a responsible coaching decision and probably helped her get to know most of the players who'd been on last year's team.

I looked up as I turned around, seeing Jake still watching us. What was up with him? Years of silence and now he was interested in what was going on in my life? I just hoped the interest hadn't come because of what was written on my notebook.

I was feeling confident as the girls made it out to the field and changed into cleats, ready for the tryout. This was the highest number we'd had in the last few years, and after seeing some of them throw, I wondered if they thought a new coach wouldn't care if they'd ever played in their life.

After a quick introduction, Coach Ambrose said, "Line up behind home plate. We'll get started with conditioning now."

From the smile on her face, this was not going to be good.

CHAPTER 4

JAKE

For some reason, I couldn't keep my mind off Penny Davis. I was lucky that the hundreds and thousands of reps I'd done throughout the year took over, because all I could think about was my next-door neighbor. Seeing her precision in pitches, I knew all those long nights of throwing against the back shed had paid off. She was determined; I'd give her that. And when she'd seen me watching her, I'd had to hold back a smile at seeing her look of shock turn to one of irritation.

For some reason, I felt a slight attraction to her. It was strange to be looking at her and suddenly curious about who she could have a crush on. But then again, I'd always been comfortable around her back when we hung out. Was it the possibility that she could be taken by some other guy now that was getting to me?

As much as I'd hoped to avoid major running at the tryouts, my teammates were right in assuming it would be brutal. We sprinted and jogged for nearly forty-five minutes to start off the day, and by the end of that, at least five of the guys had packed up and left. It was always assumed that baseball was an easy sport since the players stood around most of the time. But with a team as competitive as we'd been the past few years, conditioning helped get us through the later innings of the game.

I nearly lost my cheeseburger when Coach Maddox finally told us to grab our gloves and head out to the field. The time flew from there as I moved from station to station. When we finished up, I looked over and was surprised to see the softball girls just barely leaving their field.

Penny was walking next to some of the girls I didn't know, and I grabbed my bag, jogging to catch up with her.

"So, how'd it go?" I asked, giving her one of my biggest grins.

Her eyebrows rose, and she shifted her bat bag onto her shoulder. "What do you want, White? I think this is the most you've talked to me in years."

I shrugged. "Maybe I want to talk to you. It looks like you guys had a tough tryout." I turned my attention forward, not in the mood to gloat over the doe-eyed expressions of the girls walking on Penny's other side. This was definitely a first.

"Lots of running and then the usual drills." Her words came out clipped, as if she was just waiting for me to leave. I could take a hint, even though I wanted to badger her about who she was crushing on one more time. Why was that so interesting for me all of a sudden?

After a quick nod, I said, "Well, I hope you make it. I've gotta run, so I'll see you around the yard." I picked up my pace to catch up with Dax, who'd almost made it to the locker room.

A quick shower later, I came out to a nearly empty parking lot and threw my bag in the trunk of my new Jeep. Well, the restored version. From after the accident.

I shut the window and walked to the driver's side, hearing

a car trying to start but not turning over. I glanced to the left and found Penny with the most determined expression I'd ever seen, turning the ignition on her rust bucket.

I waited at least a minute before walking over to her. When she saw me outside, she rolled her eyes and slammed the steering wheel. A few seconds later, she rolled her window down.

"Here to gloat, White?" The sarcasm in her voice caused me to laugh, much louder than I expected.

"No, just thought I'd see if you need some help." I crossed my arms on her door and glanced in. "Sounds like you need a new car."

A fist flew at my left shoulder, connecting and leaving a surprising throbbing in its wake. "Easy for you to say. My dad can't afford to buy me everything I want."

I winced, thinking of all the strings attached to the "gifts" my parents gave me. Sure, it was nice to have an awesome SUV to drive around, but it didn't come without guilt and expectations, especially from my father.

She leaned forward and tried the ignition another time or two.

"Sorry, I'm not good with cars, but I can offer you a ride home." I stood and motioned to my Jeep a few parking spots away.

Penny frowned, her lips pursed as though she'd eaten one of those sour candies. "Did you get knocked in the head at practice today? Because you're acting really weird."

"What do you mean 'weird'? We used to do stuff like this all the time, even before we could drive. Maybe I realized how much I've missed hanging out with you." As much as I wanted it to be a line, the kind I usually fed to all the fawning girls, the truth of it hit me in the chest. There were a lot of good memories with Penny by my side, and for the first time in a while, it was like I'd woken from a strange dream and wanted things to go back to the way they were before life erupted, for both of us.

She turned the key once more and shook her head when it didn't start. Opening the door, she stepped out, her pointer finger waving before she even said any words. "The only reason I'm getting a ride from you is that I'll be late for work if I don't." She slammed her door and marched over to my Jeep, not waiting for me to join her.

We hopped into the Jeep, and I put it in drive, turning the wheel toward the exit. The sound of the radio blasted through the vehicle. And then it didn't.

I glared at Penny. "Hey, this is my vehicle. That means my radio station."

She still had her fingers on the tuner, changing it to one of the country radio stations instead of the loud metal I'd been listening to. "Not when I'm in here, it doesn't. How can you understand anything they're saying anyway? It's just a lot of loud instruments and screaming."

She tapped her foot along with the mellow beat, her mouth moving with the words, drawing my eyes to her lips. Since when did I care about the lips of Penny Davis? I'd done my fair share of kissing the girls of Rosemont High in the last two years, but I'd never had such an urge to kiss someone as I had right then. Was it that she hated me to the point where it was like pulling teeth to get her to accept a ride home? Or was it—

"Watch out!" Penny pointed to the car stopped at the exit. "This was a bad idea. Why I even thought of accepting a ride from you was a lapse in judgment on my part." She was clinging to the handlebar above the window, looking as though she was ready to hop out at any moment.

"Chill," I said, trying to calm my own heart rate. I didn't need to be in another accident, and the fact that I'd let myself get that distracted while behind the wheel had my stomach twisted in knots. "I'm not going to hurt you."

She looked at me, rolled her eyes, and shook her head. "Yeah, you've told me that before." She pulled her arms tight against her middle and frowned, her attention on something in front of us. If I hadn't known better, I'd have said she was trying to light something on fire.

I didn't want to admit it, but she was right. Years ago, she and I did everything together, and every time her parents fought, she'd come over and hide out in my room. I'd do everything I could to reassure her that I'd never hurt her, at least not like her parents did to each other. And then I'd ditched her right around the time her mother walked out. Acted like she no longer existed.

Guilt constricted my chest, making it difficult to breathe. Some friend I was. But there was a lot more to it than that. I couldn't tell her why. After everything that had happened in the few short years since, I wasn't worthy to be her friend— or anything more, for that matter.

"How many advanced classes are you taking this year?" I asked, hoping to pull my mind from the well of deep thoughts.

"Four. The more tests I can take and pass, the less I have to pay for college. I'm hoping to have an associate's by the time we graduate."

I thought about my dismal schedule and laughed. "Associate's. Do you still want to be a therapist?"

She looked at me as though surprised I would actually remember something like that. "Yep. It's a long road to get there, but I want to help people." Sadness passed over her features, and she rolled her lips in, glancing down at her intertwined fingers.

"Well, if anyone can do it, my money's on you, Pen. I'll be

lucky to graduate at all at the rate I'm going." The D plus from my last history test flashed in my mind, and I grimaced.

"It doesn't make you weak to actually try in school, Jake," Penny said. She'd turned her body toward me, leaning her head against the window as she stared in my direction.

I pulled onto our street and then turned into my driveway a few seconds later. "You sound like my mother."

Shifting into park, I caught her shaking her head and hopping out of the Jeep like it was suddenly on fire. She stomped over the small strip of grass that ran between our driveways and was almost in the house before I shouted, "You're welcome for the ride."

A sarcastic, "Thank you," rang out before the door slammed shut. I guess it wasn't possible to make up for three and a half years all in one day.

CHAPTER 5

PENNY

hankfully, I'd remembered to dry my uniform the night before, because with the delay, I was going to have to throw it on and bike to the diner. I hated being late. It was the worst thing a person could do when other people were depending on them, and I knew tonight was going to be crazy. The Rosemont Book Club usually came in on the third Tuesday of the month, and given how many ladies attended, I was usually hopping around the diner to keep up.

I threw my wallet and phone into a small drawstring backpack and redid my ponytail, smoothing back the wisps that kept flying out the sides. Running out the door, I grabbed my old bike, grateful my father took such care in maintaining things like that. He knew how unreliable my car was, but with funds so tight, this was the best option when things didn't go as planned.

As I pushed on the pedals to cross the driveway, movement from the upper window of the White house drew my attention, and I saw Jake looking down at me with an expression I'd never seen on him before. Old Jake was always transparent, but new Jake seemed to be guarding so much behind the mask of indifference and sarcasm. This look, though, was something mixed, as though he were feeling both pity and shame at the same moment.

I thought about flipping him off, but that wasn't my style, no matter how much his just leaving me behind still hurt after all this time.

Lou's Diner was a mile away from our house, and I pulled up breathless and one minute late. I parked my bike around back and ran into the kitchen, pulling an apron from the wall and tying the strings in back.

"Penny Davis, late?" came a deep rumbling voice behind me.

I turned to see my boss, Lou, flipping burgers next to the grill. "I know, I know. I had tryouts today, and then my car wouldn't start, so I had to ride my bike. I'll make it up to you, Lou." I gave him a small smile.

He waved his hand at me. "It's all good, girl. I'm just glad to see you. We've got the monthly book group in the back corner, and I'm afraid Claudia is ready to quit."

The Rosemont Book Club consisted of nearly fifteen ladies in their sixties and seventies. Each of them liked to meddle in the townspeople's lives, and I'd never met a more opinionated group of people. But they could also be the typical sweet old grandmas if shown you weren't one to be walked all over.

"Do you want me to take them from Claudia?" I asked, making sure my apron was stocked with straws and my order pad.

"Yes, please," came a feminine voice from the other side of the prep station in the middle of the kitchen. Claudia looked more frazzled than usual, her slightly graying hair looking more silver in the fluorescent lighting. "They're driving me crazy, and all I've done is bring the drinks out."

I waved a hand and smiled. "No problem. I'll go make sure we've got everything figured out."

It took about ten minutes for the women to give their order, even though it was nearly the same month in and month out. Some changed a little because they were on a diet or wanting to try something new, but for the most part, their orders were as predictable as their showing up at the diner every month.

"What book are we discussing this month, ladies?" I asked, finishing up the last order on my notepad.

"It's one Gladys picked out," Karla said, pointing to the woman at the far end of the table. The woman leaned a little closer and covered her mouth so only I could hear. "It was the most boring piece of trash I've ever read. I wish I was like some of these gals and could just pretend to have read it."

I covered my mouth to keep the rest of the group from hearing my laughter, wondering what it was about. When I got myself under control, I clicked my pen and said, "Perfect. I'll go get your meals going and be right back to fill up your drinks." The one lady at the end was always a camel, and I'd probably have to refill her glass at least four times before she left.

The bell above the door rang, and I said, "Welcome to Lou's. Take a seat, and we'll get you taken care of," before even turning to see who it was. When I turned, I stopped in my tracks, swallowing hard. "What are you doing here?"

To his credit, Jake looked just as shocked to find me in the diner as I was to see him again so soon after our ride home from tryouts.

"We decided to meet up for some food," he said, pointing to his crew of baseball friends behind him. "You work here?" The disbelief in his voice caused me to shift from one foot to another.

Deciding not to answer the obvious question, I repeated,

"Take a seat. I'll send someone out to help you," before turning on my heel and marching back into the kitchen.

I took a breath, trying to hide the burning shame that kept creeping up, heating my cheeks. I'd been working at Lou's for the last three and a half years, starting out bussing tables and then waitressing ever since. In that time, I'd only had a handful of students from Rosemont come in on my shift, and I'd always been able to avoid waiting on them. But the look on Jake's face as one nostril turned up at the thought of working in a place like this made me feel like I'd just swung and missed at a change-up.

"Claudia," I said, walking up to the middle-aged woman. "There's a group of guys out there who go to my school. Will you take their table?"

"Sure. Looks like there are five of them? Can't be worse than those ladies out there."

If only she knew.

I gave Lou the orders and helped get a few of the sides ready, knowing that prompt service would help avoid complaints—and I prided myself on good service. Any extra tips went into the large Mason jar in my closet, and I still had a ways to go to fill it.

A couple of times, I looked up and glanced out of the kitchen, where I saw Jake staring at me, a slight smile on his lips. If he hadn't looked so surprised upon walking into the diner, I would have thought he was stalking me.

Focusing on the orders and what I needed for each helped me avoid thinking about him, for a few minutes anyway. Why couldn't I just stick to thinking of him as a spineless jerk whose friend was killed in a drunk-driving accident in Jake's car? Why did my pulse race and my mind conjure up all the fantasies I'd had when I was hard-core crushing on the kid? Because as much as I told myself those were over, his sudden attention to me was throwing off my opinions of him.

I carried a large tray with several of the orders, grabbing a stand on my way out. I'd done this enough times that it felt automatic, but when I glanced in Jake's direction again, my foot caught. I dropped the stand and grabbed the tray with my now-free hand, knowing that sending a tray full of orders to the ground would be more embarrassing than I could ever get over and Lou wouldn't be happy.

"A little clumsy today? Aren't you supposed to be the all-star pitcher?" one of the boys called out, and from the sound, it was Dax. The rest of the group chuckled.

I didn't give them the satisfaction of another look. Once the tray was steady, I used my foot to kick the stand back up to where I could grab it and continued over to the book-club ladies. I gave out their orders before heading back to the kitchen with an empty tray, ready for round two.

"Looks like they need more help around this place," Jake said, his voice drawing my attention right before I walked into the back. The smirk on his face was the same he'd had for the last few years.

I knew it. He hadn't changed, but he was up to something. I just wasn't sure what.

CHAPTER 6

JAKE

I was impressed with Penny's skill at keeping everything balanced. At first, I was sure the tray was going to go toppling to the ground. I'd thought about getting up and helping her, but something kept me firmly seated. Maybe it was the fact that I was with the guys and they'd already started making fun of her.

When I'd spoken, it wasn't to say anything bad against her. I was just making a statement. But it acted as a double-edged sword, fooling the guys into thinking I was in on the jokes. Making fun of Penny wasn't something I would ever do—at least, not intentionally. Sure, I'd avoided her like the plague for years, but anytime someone had brought her up in conversation, I'd tried to give her some sort of compliment.

She reappeared with another full tray, not even glancing our direction. Some of the pieces of her auburn hair had fallen out of the tight bun-like ponytail she wore so often, and I wondered if it was as soft as it used to be. When she'd been stressed, it always helped to play with her hair, which somehow eased any tension I felt as well.

"What's wrong with you, Jake? You look like you haven't seen her in days," Dax said, slugging me in the shoulder. "Doesn't she live next door?"

"Yeah," I said, massaging where he'd hit me.

"Maybe you should ask her out. Then at least you'd get her out of your system." Colt took a sip of his water the older waitress had brought out a few minutes before.

Shaking my head, I leaned onto the table. "She's not in my system. We were friends growing up. Just leave her alone, all right?"

Nate was sitting on the end of the booth next to Ben and stood up, a smirk on his face. "Well, if you're not going to ask her out, I will. Do you think she'd go for me?" He took a few steps in the direction of the old-lady table, his swagger a tell-tale sign that he wasn't kidding.

I pushed Dax out of the booth and ran after him, pulling his shoulder back. What I wasn't expecting was a fist to come flying at my face. The impact sent waves of pain through my nose and face, causing tears to well up as it grew more intense. As an instinctive reaction, I balled my fist and gave him his own punch to the jaw, sending his head twisting to the side with a crack.

With a mischievous smile, Nate threw another punch, this time allowing me to dodge to the side and push him behind me. But instead of staying in the aisle, he plowed over the side of the booth we were sitting in, knocking over the glasses of water. The water on the table seemed to propel him even farther, and in a matter of a few quick seconds, Nate's head and shoulder crashed through the window looking out onto the street.

The restaurant paused, every pair of eyes staring our direction, every mouth agape.

I swore under my breath and ran over to Nate, hoping he

was okay. It had just been a joke like we'd done so many times before. But as I got closer and pulled two of my friends out of the way, my heart thrummed in my ears.

"I'm calling 9-1-1," Ben said, his voice reaching an octave higher than normal as I saw the thin line of blood seeping onto the back of the booth.

Please let him be okay. I couldn't live with myself if I'd gotten another one of my friends killed because of my foolish antics.

Nate moved slowly back into the booth, and I looked at the large gash that sliced from one side of his forehead and down across the bridge of his nose to the ear on the other side. Dark red blood already coated his face, and it kept dripping.

I grabbed several napkins, dabbing them around the wound and then finally holding them against it.

"Are you an idiot?" Penny's terse words caused me to turn, and she pushed me back, trying to get to Nate. She took over holding the napkins and whispered things to him, her voice more soothing than I'd ever heard it.

I stood away from the booth, looking at the aftermath of our friendly fight and knowing I was in deep. Not only had we broken a window, but would one of our key starters be okay to even play this season?

"I-I'm sorry," I stuttered, trying to process the quick succession of thoughts that sent me right back to that night nine months, two weeks, and one day ago. I ran a hand through my hair and sat down at a booth across from where Nate and Penny were. Dax and Colt moved closer to me, their expressions stunned. I glanced back at Ben as he explained the situation to the emergency people on the phone, taking deep breaths between speaking.

Flashing lights and sirens sounded, and a few seconds

later, they were outside the diner. I glanced over to Nate again. The color had drained from his face, making him look ashen and sickly.

Paramedics urged Penny out of the way, and they put Nate onto a gurney, wheeling him out the front door and into the back of the ambulance.

I hadn't even seen the police come through, but they stood in front of the four of us, their expressions just as stern as they'd been the night of the accident. "What happened here?"

I felt Dax, Ben, and Colt turn their eyes to me, boring into my skull.

"We were having a friendly scuffle, and I didn't realize I pushed him as hard as I did. He ended up sliding over the booth and into the window right there." I pointed to the spot, even though I was sure they didn't need help finding where the injury had occurred. The cracks in the glass ran all the way up, and a thick trail of blood stretched across the table.

Feeling lightheaded, I turned to study a scratch on the table in front of me. Blood still got me, even after all this time.

"Your name?" the officer asked.

I swallowed. "Jake White."

"We'll have to talk to the owner and the parents of the other boy and see if they want to press charges, Mr. White. Why don't you take a ride with us?"

I nodded, knowing that submitting would be the best option for my future. I didn't need a felony or misdemeanor on my record, or I'd never get into college. One of the officers walked in front of me to the door as the other one breathed down my neck behind me.

Remembering I'd driven, I turned and tossed the keys to Dax. "You need these more than I do right now."

Dax caught them with ease and nodded, his grim expression the same as the other two behind him.

As I walked past the long table of older women, each of them seemed to be trying to take in as much as they could so they could spread the news around town. Just what I didn't need. An audience who couldn't keep quiet.

CHAPTER 7

There had been a lot of clean-up after Jake's fight, and I was grateful the book club broke up sooner than usual, no doubt ready to go tell everyone in town what had happened at Lou's diner.

Jake hadn't changed a bit. He'd always had a bit of a temper on him, but throwing his friend through a window? That wasn't something I'd expected of him.

The other three baseball players had paid their tab, and when I walked over with a large bucket and a rag, hoping to clean up as much of the small shards of glass as I could, Dax stopped me.

"Sorry about all the mess, Nickel." His use of Jake's nickname for me caused bile to rise up my throat. I didn't even like it when Jake used it, but his best friend should have known better.

"Don't call me that. Jake's your friend. You're lucky you aren't the one in the hospital."

"He didn't mean it. He was just joking around, trying to get Nate to stop—" He clamped his mouth closed as if he'd already said too much.

"To stop what?" I asked, suddenly curious.

Dax shook his head. "Never mind. You know he can be a bit competitive, but he would never hurt someone on purpose. It was just a chain of unfortunate events."

I closed my eyes for a second and gave a mirthless laugh. "I don't know why you'd think I cared, Dax. Jake stopped being my responsibility a long time ago."

Without waiting for a response, I turned and got to work on the booth. Lou was already on the phone with the insurance company and whoever else needed to be contacted about the incident. Claudia had practically dropped at the idea of cleaning up glass and blood. As long as I was careful, I could at least make it look less like a murder scene.

Only two more hours were left of my shift by the time I finished, and it seemed word had spread through Rosemont already. We got a few customers who actually wanted food, but the rest either came inside to look at where the incident happened or congregated outside the window, talking loudly about it.

As per usual, the story had escalated to unfair proportions, but there wasn't much I could do. Jake was probably going to get some sort of probation, as long as Nate's parents didn't decide to sue him. Just one more reason I was better off steering clear of Jake White.

I rode my bike home, pulling into the driveway to lights on in every room. My dad's old truck was there, which was some relief. After all that had happened that night, I just wanted to go in, shower, and head to bed. With Dad there, I wouldn't have to wrangle Derrick into getting his homework done.

"Penny, I'm so glad you're home," my dad's voice came from around a corner as I entered the house. He appeared and wrapped me in a hug. "Where's your car?" His eyes glanced out the window.

"Still at the school. It wouldn't start after tryouts today. Jake gave me a ride home, and then I rode my bike to work."

He grabbed my face, turning it from side to side, looking for something. "Are you all right? You're not hurt or anything, right?"

I pulled at his hands gently, feeling a bit claustrophobic. We weren't the most touchy-feely family in the world, and I needed a bit more space. "I'm fine, Dad. Why the sudden concern?"

"Mrs. Montgomery came out when I was finishing mowing their yard and told me about the incident at the diner. I was worried something had happened to you, but you haven't answered any of my calls or messages." I could see the worry lines etched into his face. "I tried to call the diner, but the line was busy. I came right home just now to make sure you were all right, or I was going to head down to the diner and check on you."

"Sorry, I must have forgotten to turn the ringer back on after tryouts. You know how Coach Dean always was about phones. I turned it off just in case the new coach was similar."

My dad's arms wrapped around me once again, and this time I let him, knowing he'd probably been panicking for the past few hours.

"Steer clear of the White boy from now on, all right? Sounds like he's a magnet for trouble, and I don't want you getting hurt." He let go, and I took a step back.

"No problem there, Dad. I try to avoid him anyway."

As I glanced up at him, my dad looked through the window at the White home, his head shaking back and forth a bit. "I'm not sure what happened between you two, but it sounds like it's good you don't hang out with him anymore, with the accident and now this. Although, you might've been a good influence for him. We all know his dad isn't the best example."

"Yeah, I'm just really tired, Dad. I'm going to take a shower and head to bed. Talk tomorrow?"

When he nodded, I wasted no time in jogging up the stairs. I needed the silence to put everything together.

My dad's words echoed in my mind. I recalled those months after Jake started avoiding me, the hurt I felt at his betrayal of our lifelong friendship up until that point. Even if I'd had the chance, would I really have helped him avoid the problems he'd already been in?

I thought about Mr. White and all Jake had gone through because of him. He was a workaholic who tended to worry more about Jake's stats on the ball field than anything else. Even as a young kid, I was scared of his temper. That's probably where Jake got it from.

Not that it was my problem. I had to stay focused on the prize. A scholarship was the only way I would get away from Rosemont and create the life I wanted.

I looked at my bulging backpack on the floor and sighed. It wouldn't be a quick shower and then bed tonight. I had too much reading to get done for the next day and an essay to finish.

CHAPTER 8

"You sent a kid's head through a window?" My dad's voice on the other end of the line caused my whole body to clench, as if he'd be able to deal me another blow through the phone. I'd turned off my own phone as it seemed the gossips had already done their job spreading the news around town.

The police had dropped me off at home thirty minutes earlier after Nate's parents decided not to press charges. With Dax, Ben, and Colt's side of the story, it was ruled an accident, but we'd have to pay for the window. Which is why I had to call my dad, who was on business in Missouri.

"It was Nate, Dad. We were joking around. He punched me, so I punched him back, and when he tried again, I dodged it and shoved him. The momentum just carried him through the window."

There was a quick pause, and he said, "Well, at least you didn't lose. I'd hate to have a son who can't win in a fight."

I wasn't sure what to say. It wasn't until my father said those words that I realized how much appearances really mattered to him.

"I've already gotten a call from the owner of the diner, and they want the window fixed."

"Are you going to pay for it?" I asked, ready to be done with this conversation.

"No," he said, his voice gruffer than at the beginning of the call. "You're going to do that. You'll work off the cost of the window at the diner. Lou knows you play baseball, so he'll make sure to schedule you around practices and games. But I told him you'd be working for free until the end of the school year."

"For free?" I stood and slammed a fist into my pillow. At least it was softer than Nate's nose.

A mocking laugh sounded through the line. "Yes, for free. Just because I work hard to give you everything you have doesn't mean you're going to squirm out of anything else, young man. I got you off scot-free from the accident, even had your Jeep fixed up when the insurance wouldn't pay the full amount. But it seems you need to learn a few things about life." He paused a moment, and I fell back on the bed, knowing this was going to be the longest few months of my life.

"Jake? I've got to go. Tell your mom I'll be home next week. I've got to meet some clients for drinks. I better have no more phone calls about your behavior, you understand?"

"Yes, sir," I choked out through the anger brimming in my throat. I hung up the phone and was ready to chuck it across the room when I remembered it was my mother's. I took it back downstairs, finding her in the kitchen. "Here's your phone, Mom."

She turned around, stirring a cup of tea, the dark circles under eyes looking more prominent than they had in a while. "What did he say about the window?"

"I guess the owner already called him. Dad made a deal so I have to work at the diner for free until the end of the school year to pay it off." I spat out the last few words, feeling the injustice of it all.

"Maybe this will be good for you. Because it doesn't seem like you learned your lesson from Troy's death." She raised her eyebrows as she took a sip from the cup, her words slicing through me. I'd learned plenty from the accident, and with the nightmares that recurred several times a week, I wasn't sure I'd ever forget. "You might want to call your coach and tell him what happened. I'm sure if you wait until practice tomorrow, he won't be too happy to find out then, if he hasn't already."

I scrubbed my hands over my face. "That's just the conversation I want to have right now. 'Hey, Coach, I kind of pushed Nate through a window.'"

"Would you rather still play baseball or be suspended? Doesn't he have a no-violence policy?"

I nodded. Coach also had a no-alcohol policy he'd put into place ever since his star third baseman died driving home from a party. Even with a phone call, I might not be playing baseball this year. And that, most of all, crushed me.

When the police had gotten word to me that Nate just needed about thirty stitches and several butterfly bandages, I don't think I could describe the relief. At least he hadn't lost his sight or anything. After that worry had worn off, I'd moved on to baseball. My teammates would be furious, but my coach would be irate.

"I'll go call him right now. Then I'm heading to bed."

"Good night, dear. Make sure you stay quiet. Your sisters are already in bed."

I trudged up the stairs and past my twin sisters' room, hearing them giggling about something. Probably boys.

Turning my phone on, I lay on my bed and wrapped an arm under my head, holding it up a bit. My text message sound went off several times, most of them from numbers not saved in my phone. I clicked on the phone icon and found my coach's number. It rang a few times, and I hoped it would go straight to voicemail. My heart skipped a beat when I thought he picked up the phone, but luck was on my side.

After the beep, I said, "Hey, Coach, this is Jake. There was a little mishap today at Lou's Diner. Nate and I were joking around, and I pushed him harder than I thought, right through the front window. He'll be okay, and I've never felt worse. Just, uh, call me tomorrow."

I clicked end and chucked the phone onto my desk. Falling back on my bed, I closed my eyes, wishing for this day to end. But as usual, the demons of my past came out in full force. It was going to be another long night.

CHAPTER 9

PENNY

I wiped the sweat from my forehead and stood on the line once again, getting ready to run the next sprint. Coach Ambrose had led a decent second day of tryouts, but it had quickly turned into practice with the twenty-two remaining girls. Just like most of the coaches I'd had before, we were ending with conditioning, and combined with the Texas heat even at the end of January, my legs and chest were feeling the intensity of it.

We were set up in lines of two, paired with someone who was about the same speed we were so we "could push each other to the finish," as Coach explained. Starting from the foul pole on the first base side, we ran the warning track to get to the pole on the third-base side. I was paired with Lacey Montgomery, one of the sophomores this year, and for a minute I was sure I was going to lose, until a burst of energy surged through me and I crossed the line two steps ahead.

"Nice run," Lacey said, hands on hips as we walked back and forth, waiting for the rest of the pairs to go.

"Thanks," I said, breathing hard. "I needed the push from

you." There were times when I thought I should just quit the high school team and make sure to keep my grades up because I'd get a scholarship from my travel team anyway. The competition wasn't nearly as tough as my other team, but with the amount of work we'd already put in on day two, it seemed Coach Ambrose had dreams of taking a state title.

We ran and ran until several girls threw up on the side. My stomach didn't often get rattled, and even I was feeling the effects of the sprints.

"Okay, we're done for today," Coach Ambrose said, to a host of exhausted cheers. "Bring it in for a cheer."

Now that practice had ended, my brain turned to the rest of the evening. I was scheduled again at the diner, meaning I had to hurry. Since my car still wasn't working, I'd asked Kate to come back and get me so I could make it home with enough time and get to the diner. As I passed the baseball field, I glanced at the guys as they took grounders and fly balls on one side of the field while several were doing batting practice at home plate.

The coach tossed a ball from behind a screen to someone at the plate, and as he swung, I recognized the fluid motion of Jake's swing. I'd worked for years to get my swing to be a cheap copycat of his, yet he barely practiced but seemed to swing with ease, sending the ball into deep left field.

He turned at that moment and saw me, a bright smile on his face, before settling back into the batter's box. I caught myself swooning a bit and shook my head, stomping in the direction of the parking lot and making sure to keep my eyes straight forward. I wasn't going to let him invade my life and then drop it like he'd done so long ago.

"Hey, girl. How was practice?" Kate asked as I got into her car. "Wow, you look a little pale. Are you all right?"

"I'm fine. We just had to run a lot at the end, and I need some water." I pulled my backpack from the back seat and dug around inside, looking for the water bottle I carried around at school. Taking a long swig, I breathed in, grateful I was in a car I trusted this time.

"How was your day?" I finally asked now that my tongue didn't feel like a thick paperweight in my mouth.

Kate grinned. "It was really good. We worked on a bunch of posters for the girls' game on Friday and then started talking about prom. We haven't come up with a theme yet, but I'm so excited for it."

"Prom is, like, months away. Aren't there dances in between you have to get ready for?" Not that I was some sort of dancing expert. I'd only gone to one of the girl's-ask dances in the fall, and that was only because Kate had forced the rest of us to go. As far as the formal ones, I wasn't experienced in those.

"True. But the others are just smaller dances here at the school. With prom, we have to reserve the building it will be held in and get most of that done now, or else we'll be in the school gym just like all the other dances."

Kate had always been the outgoing one of our eclectic friend group, and Junior Class President definitely fit her. She was the most organized person I'd ever met, and I loved that she got so excited about things, even if I wasn't that into them.

We arrived at my home with a few minutes to spare, and I thanked her for the ride before running in and changing once more. Grabbing my bike, I glanced at the clock on my phone, telling myself I was going to make it to the diner in thirteen minutes this time instead of sixteen like the day before. Yes, I'm just that competitive.

"Hey, Lou," I said when I arrived, readying my apron. "How's everything tonight?"

"We've got a lot of customers. I'm thinking some of that

has to do with my large window being covered in cardboard."

I looked through the kitchen window and saw several pieces of what looked like boxes duct-taped across the opening from the day before. "Well, it looks like you got some free advertising anyway." I smiled as Lou chuckled, holding his stomach.

"Sara has already complained that customers just want the scoop on what happened before they order."

I waved him off. "It'll be fine. It's not that exciting here in town, so when something like this happens, everyone swarms to it like flies to fruit."

I turned to leave, then Lou said, "Oh, we've got a new hire that will be here in about an hour. You're training, so get ready."

"Who?" I asked. Our town was no city, and there was a chance I could know the person. At least knowing who it was would help me prep to teach them what they needed to know about working here.

"You'll just have to wait and see." The glint in his eye made my teeth clench. Lou liked surprises, but his usually turned out to be less than pleasant.

The hour passed quickly as I juggled trays of food and poured countless amounts of water and soda into glasses. The bell rang, and I turned to greet the new worker, only to see Jake White grinning at me.

"Seriously? Lou didn't ban you from this place?" I asked, setting the pitcher of water back on the waitress stand and moving past him to the kitchen.

"He probably thought about it, but I guess he wanted to get some compensation for the window," Jake said from behind me.

I stopped and turned. Lou's grin earlier came to mind, and my stomach sank. "You're the new hire?"

Jake wiggled his eyebrows and chuckled, something I used to find so funny. Right now I just wanted to knock the smug look off his face. I probably would have, too, if there weren't so many people watching.

Shaking my head, I turned back toward the kitchen and walked in, stopping a few inches from Lou. With my hand on my hip, pointing behind me, I looked up at him and glared. "Really? This is the surprise?"

Lou turned to see who I was pointing at and nodded. "Might as well get some work out of him for the damage he did to my window."

"And what if he breaks another one?"

"I'm right here," Jake said, waving.

"Better get training him. I just heard another bell, and he'll need to get some of the tables cleaned up."

I grinned, suddenly realizing I wasn't training him as a waiter but as a busboy. "I've got it from here."

After a couple steps to the rack of aprons, I grabbed one and tossed it to Jake. He caught it and stared at it a few seconds as if he had no idea what to do with one.

"It's called an apron," I said, emphasizing the words slowly and with my hands. "You wear it around your waist."

For the first time since he'd bumped into me in the hall the day before, he frowned, and the thrill of satisfaction at making fun of him didn't quite feel how I thought it would.

"I'm not an idiot, Davis." He pulled the strap around his head and started tying the strings around his waist. Once he'd finished, he crossed his arms and looked at me, eyebrows raised. "What's next?"

I focused on his words and realized I'd been standing like a statue for several awkward seconds. "Right this way."

We walked over to the large gray bins we used to collect the dirty dishes. "Take this," I said, tugging one of them free from the stack. "You'll also need a rag to wipe off the tables after you clear them."

Outside the kitchen, I pointed to two tables next to each other littered with several plates, glasses, and napkins. "Go ahead and clear all those dishes into the buckets and then wipe the tables off. I'll go check on my tables and be back to show you how to wash the dishes."

He stared at the tables as if in disbelief that this was how his afternoon would end. I left him there, seeing several glasses that needed to be refilled and several small requests from the customers. Once I'd caught up, I walked into the kitchen to find two heaping gray buckets of dishes sitting next to the large sink.

Jake stared at me, a slight hint of a smile on his lips.

This was not good. I'd managed to avoid him for the three and a half years since he'd betrayed me, and now just being around him was cracking the shell I'd built around myself when it came to him.

I pulled several of the dishes out of the bin, setting them in the bottom of the sink. "Put all the paper napkins, straws, and straw papers in the garbage," I said, grabbing several of the items and turning to drop them in the large black can behind me. Resuming my position, I pulled a scrubber from behind the faucet and turned the water nearly to hot. "Then just make sure to scrub these as best you can before placing them in the dishwasher."

"Why bother to wash them first?" he asked, taking the scrubber from me.

"Because this thing is ancient," I said, tapping on the washer, "and when it goes down, you'll have to wash and dry everything by hand to make sure it's all sanitized. It's really no fun; I promise."

His face softened, and I turned away, feeling the intensity of his gaze. "How long have you worked here?"

I turned back, surprised by the question. Instead of some sarcastic retort, I went with the truth. "Since the week after my mom left. I knew Dad wasn't going to be able to pay for all the extra activities when he had the mortgage and food to worry about." My throat felt tight, talking about something so candidly with the one person I should've been able to rely on this whole time.

He touched my forearm, the wetness from his fingers sinking into my skin and the warmth there causing my stomach to flip. "I'm sorry, Pen. I'm sure it's been hard without her."

Raising my chin an inch or two, I shook my head. "We've managed just fine. If my mother preferred the lavish lifestyle and a new family, we're better off without her." My heart knew I was lying as much as my brain tried to convince it otherwise.

Jake opened his mouth to reply, but Sara came in saying that one of my tables needed something. I nodded at Jake and left the kitchen, feeling more vulnerable than I had in months, years even. How was I going to work with him and keep my focus on the future rather than dwelling in the past?

I'd just have to make sure I kept my eyes on the prize: a scholarship to anywhere but here.

CHAPTER 10

JAKE

It took several minutes for my hands to adjust to the stinging hot water. But it somehow didn't compare to the feeling I'd had while I watched the emotions on Penny's face as she talked about her mother's betrayal. No doubt she felt the same about me, and the thought caused my stomach to sour. I'd messed up big time when it came to her. But would she ever accept my reason for turning my back on her in her time of need?

I didn't get a chance to think on it too long as the other waitress came in and said there were four other tables that needed to be cleared as soon as possible. I walked out with my gray bucket and saw several people sitting and waiting near the entrance to the diner. I thought about dropping the bucket and making my way out of there, but Penny would probably have to clean up the mess, and then where would I be at getting her forgiveness?

But why did I suddenly want her to forgive me? I thought through it as I got to work on the tables, but I didn't come to any firm conclusions.

It took nearly ten minutes to clear everything and wipe it

down, having to retrieve more gray buckets a few times to hold all the dishware. By the time I was done, I sighed, knowing I still had a lot to do on the other end.

I passed Penny a few times, and the lightness in her voice, her laugh even, made me long for those simpler times when we would hang out in the treehouse in my backyard or play catch for an hour or two. Even as I listened to her joke with the customers, something pinged around in my chest, making me feel the guilt even deeper. I'd screwed things up back then, but maybe there was time to fix it.

I'd loaded several batches of dishes through the washer and was surprised when Penny came into the kitchen and stood near me.

"How's it going? Looks like you're getting the hang of it." There were no traces of the sarcasm I'd been met with for the past two days.

"I'm surviving. It's actually not too bad, and I kind of like it." The words surprised even me, as I'd been able to escape life so far without a job of any sort. I thought back to her retort yesterday when I'd mentioned needing a new car.

Penny folded her arms across her chest, her expression bordering on triumphant. "It's amazing what you can accomplish when you put your mind to it, right?"

I dipped my head, raising an eyebrow as I asked, "What's that supposed to mean?"

"Just that. You have so many talents if you'd just apply yourself. One of your friends said you aren't planning on going to college." There was no trace of sarcasm in her voice, only a hint of disappointment. Much like my own mother's opinions.

"I never said that. But maybe college isn't the route I'm meant to take."

Reaching her hand out to emphasize her words, Penny said, "Right, Jake. Just give up like you do everything else."

Something about her words burned me, and anger rushed to the surface, heating me all the way to the tips of my ears. Doing my best to keep my voice even, I said, "Just because things got a little complicated in my life doesn't mean I give up on everything. Look at baseball. I'll still be on the all-state team no matter what happens." I omitted the state of my grades as I didn't want another emotional kick to the gut. My coach had mentioned something about getting my grades up or I would be on the bench more than on the field. But I couldn't let Penny's words get to me.

"Is that all you want? Because you have the talent, and the arrogance, to go much further than that. The way you swing the bat, scouts would be killing themselves for you to play in the higher leagues." She licked her lips, which drew my eyes to them. They looked so full and pink. If someone had told me a week ago that I'd be thinking about kissing Penny right now, I'd have thought they'd lost a few screws.

I shook my head and went back to the dishes, her words playing on a loop in my mind. "I'm not cut out for the majors."

She sighed, and when I looked over, I saw her eyes roll. "Right. If you'd just try, you might surprise yourself."

I couldn't tell her that the thought of being too far from home for an extended amount of time caused such a fear to grow inside me that it left me almost paralyzed. Leaving my mother and twin sisters alone with my father when he came home from one of his drunken binges was not something I could consider. I'd had too many nightmares that he'd hurt them beyond repair.

After a few minutes of silence, her voice came out a bit softer. "How's Nate? Did he come to practice today?"

I reflected on seeing Nate at lunch, and the same wave of guilt flooded me as it did then. Nate had been good-natured about it, with bandages covering part of his forehead and down the side of his face where the stitches were. He'd been told to take a week off from any physical activity, but if everything looked good, he'd be able to play in the home opener. I was already suspended from that game, and the only reason I hadn't been kicked off completely is because Nate and the other guys vouched for me. At least Nate didn't hold a grudge.

"He's good." I watched her expression, curious if Nate could be her mystery crush. I shrugged off that idea as I remembered a conversation with Penny in the treehouse out back about how she would never be in a relationship with someone younger than her.

Deciding to explore the subject, I asked, "What about you? Are you seeing anyone? Have a crush on someone special?"

Her cheeks flared red, and she bit the side of her lip as her eyebrows cinched together. "No. To all of the above." She turned and grabbed several plates from under the warmer, setting them on the large brown serving tray.

I couldn't let it go. "But what about your notebook? It seems you have a crush on someone."

With her eyes closed and her face tipped toward the kitchen ceiling, she took in a deep breath and let it out slowly. "Just leave it be, all right? That's ancient history."

I took a few steps toward her, wiping my wet hands on my apron. "So, it's true. The tomboy has a crush."

"Had a crush," she said harshly, baring her teeth at me. "He isn't worth my time anymore."

Without another word, she picked up the tray and turned to the door, not glancing back once.

I'd hit a nerve, which only caused my curiosity to grow even more. I'd have to watch her at school and see if there was anyone she paid particular attention to. The fleeting thought that I wished it was me caused me to chuckle out loud. She'd always been the tomboy next door, the girl I could talk to about anything until my family's problems escalated to the point where I couldn't have anyone over when my father was in town.

But the memory of her lips drew me in, and I went back to the dishes. There was no way she could like me, not with how badly I'd hurt her back in middle school. But there was a whole school full of options for her. I'd just have to see which guy drew her interest.

CHAPTER 11

PENNY

That week and the next passed with little fanfare, and I was ready for our first game against a team from the next town over. Coach Ambrose had been working us hard, and as much as I loved to hone my skills and reach the crazy goals I'd set for myself, I was sick of running like a track star.

Walking out to the field, I caught sight of Jake on his field taking grounders from his coach. It had been a while since I'd seen him put in the extra effort, even with the thing he loved the most. Maybe my conversation about him going further than one more year in high school had had some effect on him.

I continued in the direction of the softball field, my thoughts running from one thing to the next. Jake had surprised me with his work at the diner. He'd always been the one to let everyone else do all the work, but he actually stuck with it through the shifts I'd trained him without complaint.

He hadn't given up his quest to figure out who I had a crush on, though, and that was the most frustrating part. He was a dog going after a buried bone, and I knew that any conversation over two minutes would eventually move into that territory. Even at school, he'd taken to saying hello and walking with me to the classes we had close to each other.

The thirteen-year-old me would have been ecstatic to have him there, even romanticizing the walks as though he returned the crush. But I'd been jaded for too long when it came to him, and I had to stop myself from thinking there could ever be anything between us. Even if the little voice in my head still held out hope.

It took two batters to get my head in the game, but I only gave up one hit and we got the win. The team's goal was to take the state championship, and in Texas, that was something to aspire to with all the teams that worked for the same opportunity. Each win would help.

Derrick had come to the game, saving a spot for my dad, and each time I heard them cheering, it fueled me to do better, pitch faster and hit harder. I didn't notice Jake standing behind the outfield fence until after the Varsity game ended and the JV team was warming up. I had to go shag the balls for the JV girls and turned to see him smiling at me only a few feet away.

"Done with practice so soon?" I asked. When he grinned, I nodded, turning back at the sound of a ping off the bat and scooping up the ball that rolled in my direction. This was the first time the baseball coach had let them out at a normal time since that first day of tryouts.

"Coach Maddox figured we could use the rest after yesterday's win. Nice game today." He pointed to the pitcher's mound where I'd been playing several minutes before.

I looked down, dragging my cleat along in the dirt of the warning track. "Uh, thanks. It felt good to get that first game over with." For that moment, I felt like I'd been sent back in time and had my best friend back.

"One suggestion," he said, pausing to see what I'd say. And there went the good feelings just as fast as they'd come.

My gaze moved to his face, trying to decide if I wanted his advice or not. I finally nodded, and he said, "I can see your change-up from here. You need to mask it a bit more. Make it not as noticeable to the other team."

I frowned, knowing I shouldn't have let him say a thing. "What are you talking about? I struck out at least five girls on it."

He shrugged his shoulders. "Same old Penny. Getting defensive when I try to point things out. You fidget an extra couple of seconds and then show your grip of the ball to the world before you start rotating your arm around."

I bit my tongue, reflecting on a few of the instances I'd thrown the slower speed pitch throughout the game. He was probably right. He'd always been right about things like that, able to pick up on the littlest things just by seeing them once.

"You might be right about a few of them, but you weren't here the whole game," I said, my defenses rising.

"I've been here since the third inning. I told you Coach let us out extra early today." He rested his arms atop the chain-link fence and gave me a half-smile, the one that seemed to add a few more cracks into the wall I'd built against him.

"Why would you come to a game and stay that long? I'm surprised you don't have some girl hanging off your arm, waiting for you to make out with her in public." It was petty and childish, but I'd seen him locking lips with a fair share of the girls at our school.

Something passed over his eyes, and I couldn't tell if it was anger or hurt, but it was gone soon enough, leaving the cocky Jake behind.

"Most girls don't want to watch other girls playing a sport."

"Oh, and you do?" I asked, walking toward him, hoping

my voice sounded more like the challenge I wanted it to be rather than the warble I heard in my ears.

"Davis, get in here! We're about to start the game!" Coach Ambrose's voice broke the tension I felt as I stared into Jake's dark brown eyes.

I turned and ran back to the dugout, trying not to think about him watching me. Once I stopped, I couldn't tell if my heart was beating so quickly because of the short jog or because of the brown eyes still burned into my mind. I tried not to look in his direction, but it was like a magnet kept pulling me that way. He'd moved to the stands, and after talking to a few of the spectators, he walked up the road that led back to the parking lot.

Jake White was an anomaly, and if I wasn't careful, I'd be crushed just as much as when he left the first time.

CHAPTER 12

JAKE

The rest of the guys called me crazy for wanting to stay and watch the softball game after practice. Sure, I had a million other things to do before working at the diner that night. It was the first night Penny wasn't working the same shift, and I felt the draw to see her.

When I mentioned the one negative I noticed in her pitching, I'd neglected to tell her how much she'd improved over the past few years. Her speed and precision with each pitch was something I marveled at, knowing where she'd started when we were kids. And like the fiery girl she was, she was offended for a few seconds before silently agreeing with me.

It had always been like that. She'd get mad when I told her she needed to fix something, saying it was good enough. But then she'd focus on it almost to obsession until it was perfect.

I considered that while walking back to the Jeep. As I thought about our conversation that first night at the diner, I realized she'd been doing the same thing for me. Telling me to step it up, that I was better than just a kid who played baseball in high school but didn't go further.

I was only a junior. I still had time to think about all that, but I'd spent so much of the past three and a half years knowing I couldn't go far from the house that I'd pretty much crossed off college from my list of future opportunities. My mom was fragile from the last time my father had hit her, and I didn't want it to escalate.

Penny's curiosity about the girls I hung out with told me she cared, at least a little bit. So she hadn't been completely blocking me out all this time like I thought she had. There were so many layers to that girl, and I seemed to like each one even more than I had when we were younger.

"Jake, I didn't expect to see you here still." Coach Maddox's voice caused me to come back to the present.

I lifted my head and smiled. Pointing a thumb behind me, I said, "I just stopped by to watch the girls' game for a few minutes."

"I hear their pitcher is pretty good this year. Coach Ambrose was talking about some of the contacts she was working to come and check her out this season. It would be good to have a few kids head off to college in the next few years. Yourself included, Jake." Coach Maddox gave me the typical look a person of authority does when you aren't quite meeting your potential.

"A few people have mentioned that lately. We'll see. I'd need to work on my grades a bit for that."

"The school has plenty of tutors, so don't hesitate. I'd like to see you playing under the lights someday." Coach slapped me on the shoulder and said goodbye before heading to his beat-up Chevy truck.

What was with everyone trying to get me to college lately?

I drove home, took a quick shower, and headed into the diner. Lou was at his usual spot behind the grill, and he waved to me and actually smiled. I'd worked several days since the incident with the window, and he'd mostly ignored me. At least I was making progress with someone.

"How's your friend doing? The one who went through the window?" Lou asked.

"He's doing better. He got a lot of stitches, but he played in our home opener yesterday. The doctor said he just had to wear a face mask to protect them and he'd be fine. I don't think we'll get far without him."

Lou nodded and flipped two burgers on the grill. "I'm just glad it wasn't lasting damage. It would be a shame for a talent like that to get ruined."

I agreed. "Yeah, Nate is a speed demon, and we depend on him out in centerfield."

"No punishment from your coach, then?" Lou didn't look in my direction, but the words held more curiosity than accusation.

"I had to sit out yesterday's game," I said, focusing on tying the apron strings around my waist. It had been tough to take, but I understood where Coach Maddox was coming from. He couldn't have a rule against violence if he didn't issue some kind of punishment, even with how many of the guys tried to appeal his decision.

"Better get going on the tables. Claudia's in a mood because she's had to do it several times already, and we know how that goes." He gave me a small smile, and I moved to my station, retrieving a gray bucket and wash rag.

The last time I'd worked, Claudia got so overwhelmed that she ended up throwing a dish against the kitchen wall, shattering it into a billion little pieces. It was a wonder Lou kept the woman around considering how much drama she created. Lou and Penny had worked to get the food remade so it could go out to the customers while I'd been tasked with cleaning up the pieces.

Penny. She was the only girl on my mind these days. Not that I didn't have the opportunity to flirt with dozens of girls at school every day, but for some reason, that had lost its appeal. Penny's comment about me always having a girl was like driving a dagger into my chest.

My father's alcohol problem started when he'd taken his current job two months before Penny's mother had taken off, and that wasn't the only bad habit he acquired. I'd caught him texting women or calling them at random times, and I knew he was cheating on my mom. I hadn't realized how much I was turning into him, with the constant flare-ups of anger and only sticking with a girl for about a week before moving on.

No wonder Penny found me despicable. Her father was like the king of morality, although he didn't flaunt it like most. He was a stand-up guy who got his heart broken by his wife walking out on him and his two kids for her boss. In Penny's eyes, I wouldn't measure up to her father. She'd called me a waste of space at one time back when she was trying to piece together her life, when I'd avoided her for at least two weeks before she finally caught me sneaking out of my house and through the backyard that led to Dax's place.

But people could change, right? I was young and had plenty of time to make things right with the people around me. I just needed to find a way to convince them, or even just her, that I was willing to change. Because turning into my father wasn't something I wanted to do.

Driving home after my shift, I made a mental list of things I was going to change, and the first was actually getting my homework done. I wasn't completely sure why I suddenly cared about what Penny thought after so long, but she was the most real thing in my life, the one who'd call me on my bull and put me in my place. And I needed that.

63

CHAPTER 13

PENNY

The next week sped by with another two wins for us, while the baseball team won one and lost one. That had given me plenty of ammunition to fire at Jake during our one shift together, and while I could tell he was still sore about the loss, his temper didn't flare up like I'd expected it to.

Saturday came around, and I was bored. I'd already tried contacting Kate, Serena, Brynn, and Hazel, but they couldn't get together until the evening. I'd cleaned the house while my dad and Derrick worked on a yard nearby and then finished the readings for all my classes on Monday.

I grabbed my glove and cleats from my bat bag and walked outside, sitting down on the crumbling cement porch that led from the back door to the backyard. After tying up the cleats good and tight, I whipped my arm around a few times, trying to loosen up the muscles from the long week of workouts, practices, and games.

We stored several buckets to the side of our small deck, one of which was full of old yellow softballs. I pulled the bucket over to what had become my "mound," basically just a small piece of wood my father had nailed into the ground, and took a ball from the bucket. The feel of the leather under my fingers was slick from overuse, not like the soft newness of the balls we used for practices or games, but it was a ball nonetheless, and I didn't have the money to buy new ones. All my diner money had gone toward fixing my car the week before, and I was back at square one.

I lifted my eyes to the large rubber mat my father had constructed a few years before. We'd started out with a tire I had to pitch through when I'd just begun to learn the skills around eleven or twelve, but this newer model had four small holes cut out at the heights for the strike zone.

Bringing the ball into my glove, I wound up and threw the ball underhand, sighing when it went wide of the mat. I just needed to warm up. I was never as good as I was on game days, but that competitive streak ran through me, and I wanted to be as perfect as I could on each pitch, even in practice.

I went through the bucket in a few minutes and carried it with me to pick up all the balls. My mind was wrapped up in how hard it would be to create a machine that would retrieve the balls for me, when I heard footsteps behind me, causing me to jump.

"What are you doing?" I called out as I saw Jake walking toward me dressed in long basketball shorts and a short-sleeved t-shirt, his glove in hand. The shirt seemed to hug his chest and stomach, causing my eyes to linger there longer than they should have.

He shrugged, giving me that half-grin. Even though I thought I'd built up an immunity to it, the oddness of our encounters over the recent weeks left me without words.

"I heard the typical smacking of a ball on a mat and figured I'd come out and see what you're up to." He stopped a few feet away, studying his glove, and when he looked up at me, the piercing gaze of his chocolate-brown eyes made me sway a bit. I steadied myself on the bucket before picking it up and walking toward the mound again, avoiding his gaze.

"What? No video games or girls to hang out with at this time on a Saturday?" I adjusted my feet on the wooden slat, wound up, and used a newfound energy to thrust the ball toward the mat, the smack coming in even louder than before.

"I could ask you the same thing."

With a loud chuckle, I caught him off guard. "I haven't played video games since you beat me at *Mario Kart* all those years ago. And as far as my friends, they're going to do something later tonight, probably to celebrate Brynn's basketball victory in the semi-finals."

Gripping the ball deep in the palm of my hand, I let my arm circle and let go of it, watching it almost float toward the target. I loved watching the ball dance in the air before it hit the catcher's mitt, usually fooling the batter into swinging.

"Do you mind if I catch a few?" Jake asked, moving between me and the rubber mat. He crouched on his haunches, his glove poised on one of the corners of the home plate before him.

What was I going to say? No? When I had someone who would throw the balls back to me, I couldn't really pass that up.

I threw the same pitch, a bit disappointed that it ended up two inches away from the corner. Ball.

Jake threw it back, his arm moving and all the muscles flexing at the same time. Distracted, I almost forgot to catch it and was glad my reflexes moved fast enough for me to snag it without looking like some beginner.

"You're still making that extra movement I was talking about at the game the other day. When you play against the bigger schools, they're going to notice and wait for it."

My attention snapped back to his face instead of his body, a flame of irritation igniting in my stomach.

I threw again, and Jake shook his head. "Same thing."

Suddenly wishing he hadn't invited himself over, I said, "I don't get what you mean. I'm doing everything I do with all my other pitches."

Jake strode to me, and when he stopped in front of me, it took a moment to catch my breath. What was my problem? This was Jake White, the kid who'd betrayed me, left me to fend for myself through the darkest times of my life, and my body was now the traitor.

He moved behind me, his arms covering mine and leaving a trail of goosebumps. His left wrist held mine on the glove hand, and his right hand covered my hand with the ball. When he spoke next to my ear, I felt the tingles all the way to my toes.

"Start like you normally do." He brought my hands together, hiding the ball in the glove. "When you go to rock back, your hand moves an extra couple of seconds before you even move forward." He moved my hand a couple of times and then pulled my arm back in the regular motion.

"Okay," I said, unable to move a muscle after he let go of my arms. It took everything within me to focus on what he'd been trying to tell me and not the way he smelled like guys deodorant and something like the beach.

I pitched another one and glanced over at him. Big mistake as my stomach flipped itself over from the bright smile on his face.

"Yes! That was it. Now just make sure to do that one every time."

"Sure. Easy." I tried to make my voice sarcastic, but I was pulled in by the way his eyes stared into mine.

He resumed his spot behind the plate, and I took a deep

breath. I'd done this with him so many times back in the day. Why did this time feel so different?

Probably because at the age of thirteen, Jake hadn't filled out yet. He'd shot up several inches during seventh grade and still had that gawky, skinny-teenager look to him. I'd thought he was cute then, but this new filled-out physique seemed to be making my nervous system lose complete control of its responsibilities.

I threw a couple more pitches, feeling as if my brain was sucking away all the energy I had just to get the ball forty-three feet to him and get it to hit a decent spot.

"Riseball," I said, flipping the ball in my hand as my fingers found the grip. It was the one pitch that threw every baseball player off as it was nearly impossible for their pitchers to throw something that broke upward when throwing overhand. I'll admit I needed a little ego boost after his critique.

"So you mean a fastball that doesn't break?" Jake asked, that cocky smile flashing at me again.

I opened my mouth to say something, but nothing came. Better to just show him how far I'd come.

My leg came forward at the same time as my arm, landing to give me the momentum to spin the ball up. The ball started on a flat plane and then broke upward toward the last two feet before it got to Jake. He didn't see the movement until too late, and his glove missed completely. The ball knocked against his forehead near his hairline, and he tumbled backward, leaning against the rubber mat.

"Oh my gosh! Are you okay?" I dropped my glove and ran over to him, hesitating to touch him. Four years ago, I wouldn't have given a second thought to helping my best friend and next-door neighbor, but now, things seemed different. There were still tingles on my arms from where he'd helped demonstrate what I was doing wrong a few minutes ago, and I could only imagine what would happen if I touched him again.

Jake rubbed his forehead with his hand, his one eye closed. "Since when did you get the ball to break like that? I don't remember your riseball moving so much."

"It might have been my favorite pitch to practice after you stopped hanging out with me. Now it's my best pitch." I gave him a small smile, my gaze alternating between his forehead and his deep brown eyes. "I've got a few ice packs in the house. Do you want to come in and get one? Or do you want me to bring it out here?"

Jake paused a few seconds, and part of me wondered if I'd interpreted this weird relationship wrong from the start of the day.

"I'll just wait out here."

I turned and ran inside to grab an ice pack from the freezer. Grabbing a towel from the kitchen, I wrapped it around the cold pack for insulation. Then again, with how he'd made fun of me just before I pitched it, a little frozen skin might do Jake some good.

"Here, let me see it," I said, kneeling in front of him.

He pulled his hand away, and I had to school my expression. The large bump poking out from his head was already turning colors. "Just put this on it for a few minutes. You'll have a battle scar. I should've just told you to move."

A weak smile and a deep chuckle caused me to laugh back. "I thought I could handle anything Penny Davis threw at me. I guess we just proved you have more secrets than you led on."

I sat next to him, surprised by the small amount of excitement I felt at his compliment. I pulled at the grass around me, staring at the blades of green in my hand before tossing them in the air. "Not really secrets. Just a girl trying to get a scholarship."

"A scholarship is really that important to you, huh?" The way his one eye stared into mine made me grateful I was sitting.

"My life isn't all cake and ice cream like yours. I work to pay for most of my activities, and when I'm not working, I'm either practicing or studying so I can actually get out of this town when we graduate."

His smile faltered, and he looked away. "I can understand that. But you still have a happy family, right? I mean, it's got to be easier now than it was when your mom was here."

I stiffened. I'd never really talked about my mother to anyone but Jake. The months before she finally walked out seemed like they'd never end, with the constant screaming and fighting about the littlest things. I'd spent a lot of time over at Jake's house during those days, creeping back into the house when she'd driven off or I knew for sure she was asleep.

"Yeah, that's true. I just feel bad for my dad. He's such a good guy and deserves to be happy too. Instead, he's stuck trying to provide for two kids and barely sleeps because he's always taking on extra jobs to keep up with the mortgage or the bills." As much as I didn't want it to happen, sometimes I wished my dad would just sell the house so he wasn't working himself to an early grave. But he'd already taken a hit to his pride when Mom walked out. Losing the house would be something he wouldn't make it back from.

"Well, your family looks a heck of a lot happier than mine." He pursed his lips, not meeting my gaze.

I reached over, touching his arm with my fingers. Electricity shot through me. "What happened? Your family was always happy too. Remember all the cookouts we'd have between our yards and the fun nights out our moms would plan?"

He nodded, looking more sad than happy at the memories. "Those were some good times. But then things changed. My dad got that promotion, and it was like our world just turned out to be a fake, you know?"

I opened my mouth to say something, when I heard the back door screech open. My head snapped in that direction, and I saw Derrick coming through with my father close behind.

"Penelope Davis, what is going on?" It was the sternest expression I'd seen from my father in years, and panic sank into my limbs. His earlier words to stay away from Jake popped into my thoughts, and I knew that Jake holding an ice pack to his head while we sat next to each other was definitely not something he thought he'd see.

Jake and I stood up together, and I brushed my hands off on my shorts, trying to find the words to explain the situation and make it look less, well, worse than it was.

"I was practicing out here—"

"It's my fault, sir," Jake said, cutting me off. "I came over and thought I could catch one of Penny's riseballs and ended up with a big lump on the head instead."

The anger melted from my father's expression, and within seconds, he was laughing harder than I'd seen in forever. "That pitch is wicked. You're a brave man for even standing in the line of fire without equipment on."

I turned to Jake, seeing him chuckle a bit as the mound on his forehead stuck out, reminding me it was my fault. So much for Dad going postal on the kid.

"I'm going to grill some burgers for dinner," my dad said, turning to walk back to the house. "Make sure you check for signs of a concussion, Jake. I know how much you mean to your team, and it would be a shame if you lost the game against Croydon next week."

"I hope that turns black," Derrick said, laughing and pointing as he moved to get something out of the shed.

I waited several seconds before turning to Jake, not quite sure what to say next. "I'm sorry about your head. I just hope it doesn't ruin any of your Saturday night plans. If anything, you might get more girls ready to make out with you in sympathy with this." I reached up and lightly tapped the exposed bump, trying to hide a smile when he jumped back.

"Really? Who pokes a forming bruise?" He slapped the ice pack back over the spot and frowned. "And contrary to popular belief, I don't kiss every girl I meet."

Folding my arms across my chest, I bit my tongue, willing the words not to spill out. But I didn't have that kind of willpower for long. "Could have fooled me."

Jake held up his hands, giving me the ice pack. "This was a bad idea. I was hoping we could be friends again, you know, like we used to be. At least I know your father doesn't completely hate me."

"What do you mean by that?" My defenses rose, ready to punch him if he said anything bad about my father.

"He's barely acknowledged me over the past few years. It's just nice to see him smiling at me again."

I balled my hand into a fist and slugged him in the shoulder. "I think he always thought of you as a son. When things went south between us, he turned into a protective bear. I can only imagine this looked a lot like the past, when things were simpler."

Jake looked at me, his eyes searching my face, a softness in his features that I hadn't seen since a few weeks before my mother had taken off. Were all the memories invading his brain like they were mine?

I felt the sarcasm drain away, and it made me feel vulnerable, something I'd never wanted to happen in front of him again. The attraction I now felt for the boy in front of me went way beyond what I'd tried to bury over the last few years. He was all wrong for me, and yet, there was still that goodness under the bad-boy exterior he tried to show the world.

"I better get home. But I'll see you around, Davis." He winked at me, and the effects were paralyzing. He'd made it to and around the wooden fence that separated our yards before my hand was able to rise up and wave.

My insides were on fire as I thought about all that had happened in the space of twenty minutes. How was I going to survive if I liked him as much as I was beginning to? He was Jake White, playboy of Rosemont High and ultimate betrayer of my trust. But those little peeks into his life reminded me so much more of the boy he'd been before that I wanted to trust him again, wanted to spend more time with him.

Maybe I was just a glutton for punishment.

CHAPTER 14

JAKE

I couldn't believe I'd gone over there and tried to relive something we'd had before. It was selfish, and I ended up with a large dark bruise by Sunday afternoon. I'd been thinking about Penny almost constantly since I left her backyard, and it all seemed surreal, like someone had bridged the gap of three and a half years when Penny and I hadn't talked to each other.

She had a right to be surly after all she'd been through, but there was a moment there at the end when I saw the old Penny, the one who was game for whatever adventure I proposed. The one who would forgive me for all my faults.

Was that the reason I felt so attracted to her? I missed the life I had before my world started caving in? I wasn't exactly sure, but I knew I needed Penny in my life, whether it was just as a friend or otherwise. She kept me grounded, didn't let me get too full of myself, and she reminded me that planning for the future was worth a bit of time and effort. I just needed to find a way to apologize.

I was hanging out in my room Sunday night with my

music on, tossing a ball in the air, when my mom knocked on the door.

"Someone's here to see you." She gave me a curious smile, probably because people coming to visit me at home never happened.

She stepped back and disappeared down the hall, leaving the hall empty for several seconds. I sat up, wondering if I was supposed to head downstairs, but Penny came around the corner, her eyes darting around my room as if taking in everything that had changed over the years. I'd put up a couple of new posters and had a few more trophies from our summer baseball team, but other than that, it was about the same.

"I didn't think I'd see you here anytime soon," I said, lying back down. I tossed the ball up in the air again, barely missing the ceiling.

"I brought you these."

Turning my head, I saw a plate covered in tin foil. Baked goods.

I jumped up and took the plate, peeling off the foil. "Homemade cupcakes? You made these for me?"

Her jaw shifted, and she gave a curt nod. "I just wanted to say I was sorry again about hitting you yesterday." From the tone of her voice, she wasn't completely convincing.

I peeled off the paper of one and took a large bite, giving a small sigh at the chocolate cake. It had been a while since my mother had cooked, let alone baked, and I couldn't help shoving the rest of it in my mouth.

The disgusted look on her face caused me to laugh, causing little bits of cake to get stuck in my throat. Pounding on my chest, I finally got them to pass.

"Your dad sent you over, didn't he?"

"No!" she said, folding her arms and glowering at me.

After a few seconds, her gaze dropped to the ground. "He might have mentioned something, but I made the cupcakes."

I nodded. "Well, I have to say your baking skills have definitely improved since that one time you almost lit the kitchen on fire baking a pie."

She took in a deep breath, and when she spoke, it was like she was trying to get out everything before she lost her nerve.

"Did I do something to make it so we weren't friends anymore? Because I've been going over and over what happened between us for the past three and a half years, and I still haven't figured out what I did to push you away. If anything, those first few months after my mother left were the ones I needed you most." Her voice broke on the last few words, and I couldn't look at her. Seeing the raw emotion of the hurt I'd caused was too much.

I picked up another cupcake, taking a large bite of it. After sitting on the bed, I raised my eyes to hers. For a moment, I considered spilling all the details that led to my ghosting her. But as I thought of the sickly yellow bruise still visible on my upper rib from the last time my father was in town, I knew I wasn't ready. There was no way I was ready to share that humiliation with anyone, even one of my oldest friends.

With a quick shrug, I said, "I don't know, Pen. I was an idiot. Can't you just forgive me so we can be friends again?" My words came out with more exasperation than I'd wanted, and I watched as her jaw tightened and her eyes narrowed.

"Don't choke." It was a whisper, but for some reason, it was worse than her yelling at me. She turned on her heel and left without another word.

"Way to go, Jake," I said out loud. The best chance I'd had at rekindling our friendship, and I'd botched it. That might as well be my middle name these days.

CHAPTER 15

JAKE

*M*onday morning, I threw a hat on, knowing I'd get a million questions about what had happened to my head. The brim rested right on the bruise, the discomfort making it uncomfortable at first. But my stubbornness to wear it got me through until I barely recognized the pinch of pain.

I'd gotten to school just as Ms. Lovell opened her classroom. We had an essay due on Wednesday, and I figured the best way to answer my questions was to ask the teacher herself.

Once I left her room, about ten minutes before the first bell, I saw Dax over by one of the large pillars that made up the commons area.

"We missed you at the Montgomerys' party, man. What happened to you on Saturday?" Dax asked as he reached out his hand. We clasped hands and gave each other a bro hug before resting back against the wall.

"It was just a long day. I wasn't up to a party." To be honest, I'd forgotten about it.

Dax shook his head. "The whole thing was crazy. Probably a good thing you skipped it since you've already talked to the police enough in the past month."

I turned to look at him. "Let me guess. The police showed up and arrested several people."

"Yup," Dax said, glancing over the common area. I hadn't been at school early enough all year to walk through there in the morning. "There's Jen's group. We should go say hello."

Jen Stephens had been on my radar a month ago, and I'd been working on angles to hang out with her for quite some time until, well, until I'd bumped into Penny that day before class. Had that been the turning point?

I still had no idea who the writing on her notebook referenced, and a part of me was dying to know, while the other hoped I never would. Because if it wasn't me, it would hurt more than a punch to the gut from my father.

"I'm good. Let's just sit over here. There's Ben. Where are Nate and Colt? Are they here yet?" I scanned the large room but came up empty.

"I just got here too, man. I think Nate had an appointment with the doctor this morning, though."

I swallowed a large mound of bile in my throat. It didn't matter how much time passed, I'd probably always feel guilty for what happened with Nate and the window at the diner.

At that moment, I saw Penny walking with two other girls who looked familiar. One of them played basketball, and the other was one of the student body officers. But what I noticed most was Penny's hair half-down. She'd worn it up in a ponytail for so long that I hadn't realized she'd grown it down to mid-back. The coppery waves bounced along as she walked. She wore a white blouse and skinny jeans, causing me to stare longer than I should have at her curves. She was no longer the stick from our youth.

"What's your problem, man?" Dax asked, hitting me in the chest.

"What do you mean?"

Dax frowned. "You were practically salivating over Penny Davis. Do you like her?"

"No, of course not. She's my neighbor. I guess I was just surprised she had her hair down for once." I stole a peek of her again, and it seemed Dax had done the same.

"Yeah, you're right. I've never seen her with anything but a ponytail."

I sensed Dax turning back to me, poised to ask questions, and I just hoped it wasn't anything about why I no longer had an interest in Jen Stephens. Because then I'd have to admit my feelings for Penny were growing.

I turned it over in my mind several times, and although it was selfish, I didn't want to do anything until I was sure something could work between me and Penny. I just needed the opportunity to finally tell her I wanted to try and go back to the way things had been before. But that might jeopardize my current relationship with the rest of my friend group. They were all about the partying and being seen by everyone, whereas Penny preferred to keep her head down and work to get out of Rosemont.

The bell rang, pulling me out of my thoughts, and I was actually somewhat relieved to be in class instead of getting the third degree from Dax. Life had gotten so complicated in the last three weeks, and I wasn't exactly sure how to handle it.

The day sped by, as did Tuesday, and then I was out on the field, warming up for a big game against Croydon. I felt good, like today was going to be an awesome day. The ball was launching off the bat with ease, and I'd been able to smoothly field anything Coach Maddox hit at me.

Fast forward to the middle of the game, and I was standing out at shortstop when I looked up to the stands and was surprised to see Penny sitting there in the bleachers. Her friend—Kate, I think her name was—sat next to her, the two of them talking about something and smiling. Penny's hair was pulled back now, probably because she'd been at practice before, but seeing her up there gave me a new motivation for the game.

I hadn't wanted to impress anyone as much as I wanted to at that moment, and I focused as Ben pitched the ball, the slider breaking toward the ground and faking out the hitter as he swung and missed. I slammed my fist into my glove, moving my feet back and forth to stay loose.

The next pitch came, and the batter connected, sending the ball to my side of the field. I kicked my legs into gear, ready to field the ball, when Logan Hardwick, our third baseman, fielded it cleanly and threw it over to first base, getting the guy out.

I cheered and gave Logan a high-five with our gloves before jogging over to get back in place. Ben walked the next batter, causing me to shift closer to second base in case the guy decided to steal. The first pitch to the next one was hit, too far for Logan to get this time. I sprinted as hard as I could, diving to stop the ball before it continued to the outfield. I pushed up onto my knees and turned to throw the ball to second, getting the runner out by a step.

Three outs. I heard the crowd go wild, and I stood, dusting myself off and trying to keep the wide grin off my face. I looked up to where Penny was sitting and was surprised to see her clapping and smiling back at me. Was she actually cheering for me?

I ran into the dugout, ducking a bit as the guys starting slapping me on the back, our normal custom for a great play. I leaned against the fence closest to the stands and clapped my hands together, more pumped than I'd been in quite a while. I loved this game, and I loved that someone I cared about had actually shown up to support me in it.

CHAPTER 16

PENNY

I'd thought about going home after practice, but I was so burned-out on homework that I decided to stay with Kate and watch the boys play against Croydon. It was always a tense matchup. Kate had been assigned as one of the officers to support the team, so at least I wasn't alone.

It would be easy to lie and say I wasn't watching the shortstop closely, thinking about the closeness we'd shared the other day in my backyard. Or about the way his lie to explain the distance that sprang up between us at thirteen had caused the curiosity to flow rather than making me angry. He'd always looked at the ground and shrugged when he was lying, and it seemed like that hadn't changed in all this time.

I hadn't had much time to talk to him since then, even though we'd worked the same shift at the diner the night before. The place had been so busy that it was hard to say more than "Hi" and "Excuse me."

And then he dove, showing off his athletic ability that some would only ever dream of having, making the play look like it was no big deal. Something like that would have taken me months of practice to perfect, and I knew for sure that Jake no longer practiced outside of team practice. Definitely an advantage to not being a pitcher.

I couldn't help but clap, and seeing him look in my direction caused my breath to hitch. As much as I wanted to know what his expression meant, I had to convince myself it meant nothing.

I'd seen him walking the halls with a different girl every week, and I was not going to be one of his conquests. But he'd been so different, so vulnerable during the moments I'd spent with him over the past few weeks.

"That was awesome!" Kate shouted above the cheers in the rest of the stands.

"Yeah, it was!" I said, matching her volume.

The audience settled down and got ready for the bottom half of the inning to begin. Logan, the third baseman, was first up to bat. He was a year or two younger than us, and I didn't know much about his skills except that his swing always hesitated a second too long before he swung, making it difficult to connect.

Kate tapped my leg and gave me a look that I knew meant she was going to ask me a question I didn't want to answer.

"I'm so glad you stayed to watch with me, but I have to ask. Does it have something to do with Jake White?"

I frowned, hoping to cover the sudden rush of heat to my cheeks. "What are you talking about?"

"Well, it's just that every time we've talked in the past week or two, you've said something about him, and I was just curious if you were developing some stronger feelings for him. Didn't you used to like him?"

Blowing out a breath, I stared out at the field, cringing as Logan stared at the third strike. I'd rather run out and play instead of sitting here with all the questions I was bound to get from her. But the great thing about Kate was that she wouldn't make fun of me.

"It's so complicated right now. I've been mad at him for years, and all of a sudden he's been going out of his way to say hi and be nice to me again, as if he's trying to go back to the way we used to be friends before he ditched me. I wish I could say I felt nothing for the guy, but when I see those glimmers of his former self, I go right back to being a tween crushing on the boy next door."

Clapping her hands together, Kate looked like she was over the moon. "Yay for you finally liking someone again. I know Johnny Goodman moving was hard. I was beginning to think you'd never be interested in anything but dead men from history again."

I laughed at that. I had a few historic heroes and might have talked about them more than most over the past few years. "Thanks for that, Kate."

"It's true. And I've seen Jake glance up here more than once. What if he has feelings for you too?" The joy on Kate's face made me pause for a moment. I'd focused on my future for so long that to actually enjoy the moment suddenly scared me.

"Let's be honest, Kate. We know his reputation. I refuse to be one of the girls on his long list of conquests. He'll get bored and move on anyway." The words ripped at my chest as I said them, but that was the reality of liking the bad boy. There was no happily ever after when it came to guys like him.

But could he go back to being the guy from before my mom left? The consoling one who cared about how things were going in my life and who I could talk to about anything, even the harder stuff?

He acted like I'd built a wall to keep him out, but he was the one who refused to open up about why he'd suddenly ditched me to drink and party with his friends. And with the car accident and then Nate's face going through the window at the diner, I was better off steering clear of him. Not to mention his apparent willingness to stay in town forever. There would be plenty of time to find someone when I got to college.

Even as I thought it, I watched him pick up a bat and slide on a batting helmet before taking a few swings in the on-deck circle. Gosh, why did he have to look so attractive doing that?

CHAPTER 17

JAKE

I saw Penny walking through the halls after lunch that Friday, but before I could say anything, two of her friends joined her, Kate and a tall blonde. Kate was in one of my classes and had been extra nice to me, even more so since the baseball game on Tuesday. I hoped I wasn't attracting her attention, because that would just mean more awkwardness between me and Penny.

"Come on, Pen. You've got to get out once in a while. This is a low-key party at the Jeffersons' tonight." Kate was pleading, and I chuckled. As I thought about it, I'd never seen Penny at any party. Not that it meant a whole lot, but it was probably why it'd been easy to avoid her for such a long time. Once I stopped talking to her, we didn't hang out in the same places. Until now with the diner.

"Do it for me, Penny," the tall blonde girl said, her voice an exaggerated whine.

Shaking her head, Penny's long ponytail bounced again, captivating my attention for several seconds. I almost reached out to touch it but knew that would be overstepping.

"Can't we do something other than a party? We could rent a

movie and just hang out at someone's house." Penny's right hand held her left shoulder, something she'd always done when we were younger to signal she was uncomfortable with something.

Kate stopped in front of her, and I turned my head, trying to look like I wasn't aware they were there. "What if we go for a little bit, and if you want to leave, I'll head out with you?"

"Ugh, you two. You know how I feel about loud music and crazy drunk people."

"You'll be fine," the blonde said, rolling her eyes. "I've got to run to Trig. See you after school."

Kate and the other girl took off in different directions, leaving Penny with her head tipped back, looking like she was dreading life.

"What's got you so annoyed, Davis?" I asked, making sure she heard me before I moved into her line of sight.

She looked at me and shook her head. "You. What do you want now, White?"

"Just didn't want to see a friend looking like the world was ending. Anything I can do?" I stuffed my hands into my pants pockets, hoping to pull off the appearance that I hadn't been listening.

Penny folded her arms, her eyebrows shooting up. "Friends, huh? You'll claim me as a friend now?"

A bitter taste took over my tongue, and I swallowed several times, hoping to get it to disappear. "Can't you forgive a guy already for being a jerk? I'm sorry, and I really am. I shouldn't have pushed you away when I did."

She took a few steps forward, and I fell into step with her. "It's hard to forgive when you don't know the reason the person dumped you like a sack of garbage on the curb."

Fair point. "I know I hurt you, and I've never been more sorry about anything in my life. If I could go back and change it, I would. But I need just a little more time before I can completely confess why I did it. Is that okay?"

"Whatever. Just don't expect the same title from me until I know what happened. I've had enough people walk out of my life. I don't need it to happen twice from the same person."

I opened my mouth to say something, but for the first time in a while, I had nothing. My mind was blank.

She jutted her thumb down the hall. "I've got to get to class. I'll see you at the diner, I guess."

There was a sadness to her tone, and I wanted to reach out and grab her hand and tell her everything right then. But something held me back. Probably the fact that she was like the light, and my life had been in darkness for so long.

I watched her walk away until she moved into the classroom and the bell rang. So much for changing when it came to school. I was still going to have to work off those tardies and soon.

* * *

"WHAT ARE WE DOING TONIGHT?" Colt asked as we all got dressed in the locker room after the last bell.

"My dad is taking us camping, so I won't be around for the weekend," Logan said, looking less than enthused about the idea.

Dax turned to look at me, and I shook my head. "I don't know. What do you want to do?"

"I heard there's a party tonight. We should go and see," Dax said, a wide grin showing off his teeth.

I'd nearly forgotten about the party Penny's friends had mentioned as my thoughts had been consumed with telling her about past pain.

"I'd be down for that. I heard someone say it's at the Jeffersons' house, right?"

Colt and Dax nodded at the same time. "I'm in," they said simultaneously.

I could do with another chance to see Penny outside of softball and the diner. Maybe I'd be able to tell her everything soon enough. That is, if she trusted me enough to believe it.

CHAPTER 18

"I don't need more makeup, you guys," I said, pushing Brynn's hand away. They'd deemed tonight to be about a makeover for me, but what I really felt like was a floozy. I'd already nixed the clothing combinations they'd picked out for me.

"There is no way you're going to a party in jeans and a t-shirt." Kate's face had that no-nonsense look on it. I knew not to argue with that.

I stood from the edge of my bed and walked to the small walk-in closet. I pulled two of my "nice blouses" from the rack and held them up for the girls to see. "What about these?"

"That one looks like my grandmother's wallpaper," Serena said, going back to studying her nails.

Shooting her a glare, I hung up the one she'd been referring to and looked down at the one in my hand. It was a black three-quarter-sleeve boho-type shirt with gems and sequins throughout.

"Not bad, Pen," Kate said, pausing in reapplying her mascara. "When did you get that one?"

I tried to find the words, but it seemed my mind had no real explanation. It had been one of my mother's shirts, one of the many she left behind when she'd gone to start her new life. With the other guy. Dad had done a massive overhaul of his closet when he realized she wasn't coming back, and I'd managed to grab a few things I'd always liked.

Not that I'd ever worn any of them, but as much as I hated her still, a part of me missed what we'd had in those shining moments when she'd wanted to be a mom.

"It's been in there for a while," I said finally, blowing out a breath. Kate was the only one who knew even a sliver about my mom, and I didn't want to have to tell the entire story to the rest. I wasn't ready for that yet.

My thoughts turned to what Jake had said earlier at school. Maybe whatever he'd been through was just as bad as when my mom left, too painful to talk about just yet. We'd always been able to talk about everything, but I was beginning to realize that some of life's problems take much longer to process than others.

"Put it on, Penny," Serena said, bouncing on my bed a few times.

I slipped into the closet and pulled on my one pair of skinny jeans that Brynn had made me buy the previous summer. The blouse fit comfortably around my sides, feeling much more comfortable than the skin-tight shirt they'd wanted me to wear originally.

I walked out of the closet, not even trying to pose. If they weren't going to agree to this ensemble, I wasn't going to the party.

"That looks way good!" Kate said, clapping loudly.

"With your hair done, you look like you're in college." Brynn grinned, waving me over with the curling iron in her hand. She'd taken the time to style my hair, which was taking much longer than the last time I'd actually done it. Probably because there were several more inches than before.

Serena stood and grinned. "Yay for Penny finally joining us for a night out."

I turned as much as I could with my hair twirled around a hot iron and pointed to her. "If there's anything off after fifteen minutes, I'm gone."

The girls chuckled and gathered their things. Brynn sprayed my hair with a cloud of hairspray once again and used a comb to smooth back some of the sides. Looking in the mirror, I almost did a double-take. It wasn't like we'd had an all-day makeover, but the little makeup I'd agreed to let them apply actually accentuated several features of my face, and I couldn't help but smile.

I'd never been into makeup. I'd always thought my mother caked it on, and since I was usually out running with the boys while growing up, it would have smeared, melted, or been wiped off, defeating the purpose. But I could enjoy a little bit for one night.

We climbed into Kate's new SUV and headed in the direction of the school. The Jeffersons had a son who was a senior, and when they threw a party, I'd heard it was epic. Okay, maybe not epic-epic, as any gathering at the Montgomery place was considered something that couldn't be replicated. That was what Serena said anyway.

As we got closer to the larger home on the other side of town, my stomach twisted into knots, and I felt like I was running out of air. I pushed the button to roll down the window a bit and enjoyed the fresh air coming in. Slow, deep breaths helped to untangle some of the knots.

"I hope James is there," Serena said, her fingers tapping the screen of her phone with an intensity I'd only seen from her during volleyball games.

"Didn't you already go on a date with him?" I asked, turning my face back to the window.

The girls chuckled, and I turned to see them staring at me.

Serena rolled her eyes. "That wasn't a date. He invited a bunch of other people to tag along. But I'm determined to get an individual date this time."

"This is why you need to hang out with us more, Penny," Brynn said from the passenger seat. "It isn't the same when you're not here."

I sighed and nodded. "Thanks for being patient with me. I know I'm not the easiest person to hang out with all the time."

"We've all got our thing. Sometimes we just have to branch out." Kate smiled at me through the rearview mirror, and something in her eyes gave me an assurance that I'd be okay. From what or at what time, I wasn't sure, but it was a relaxing feeling I hadn't had in longer than I could remember.

Cars were already lined up down the street and in the cul-de-sac where the Jeffersons lived.

"Looks like we're going to be walking a bit, girls," Kate said, turning the wheel to head back to the end of the street where a spot had been open.

"This always happens when I choose to wear heels," Serena complained, sticking her phone into a small black clutch.

Brynn laughed. "At least you can wear heels. I already tower over most of the student body at Rosemont. To add heels to that would be like watching a circus performer."

We all burst out laughing at that as Kate parked the car. Getting out and looking down the road at the large house helped sober me. Why had I agreed to this?

As if reading my thoughts, Kate grabbed my arm and

gently pulled me behind the other two girls. "You'll be fine. Just relax and have fun. I'll be with you the whole time," she whispered.

As much as I trusted her, she was the complete opposite of me with a big crowd. It was as though her already outgoing personality got kicked up several notches and my social awkwardness only got worse. One of the reasons I stuck to my small group, the softball field, and books. I felt more confident in those situations.

Walking in, I could smell bodies and something I couldn't name just then. I rubbed at my nose, hoping to keep the gag reflex from kicking in.

As soon as we were inside, Brynn and Serena disappeared through the crowd, and I stood there wondering if I'd be better off just walking back out.

"Come on. Let's get something to drink and find a spot to watch. That's sometimes the best part." Kate's grin put me at ease somewhat, but I knew I was going to need more than that to last longer than one of the screaming songs in the next room.

She led me to the large kitchen where the bar was covered in bowls of ice, drinks of every kind sitting in them. I located the water and soda section and grabbed a water, already feeling the dryness taking over my mouth. The heat in the house from all the people seemed to suck the moisture right out. I pulled out my phone and took note of the time. Had it really only been three minutes? I might not even make it to fifteen at this rate.

Kate started talking to a girl I barely recognized, a senior. And just like that, I was on my own. I glanced around, unsure of what to do, and then decided to go find somewhere to sit. I passed the room with the loud head-banging music and grimaced as I watched a couple make out against the wall. What was I even doing here? This was fun?

I found the doors to the pool out back and walked outside to a chair, enjoying the refreshing air as much as I had on the drive over. All of this was something I'd never had interest in, not since my mother began telling me stories of her high school days. She would fit right into this scene, and just like all the other times, I wondered how she and my father really got together. He was so mild-mannered, although driven, and it seemed like they'd come from worlds apart to marry.

Thinking of my father, he would kill me and then bring me back to clean up the mess if he ever found out I'd had a party with alcohol. Kate had said something about the Jefferson parents being on a three-week trip to Europe. I just hoped I'd get out before the neighbors called the police.

There were only a handful of people milling around outside since a cold front had moved in during the day, making it chilly for the ones who were only half-dressed.

"I never thought I'd see the day when Penny Davis would be at a big party like this." Jake's voice caused me to jump, and I turned to see him smiling over me.

"More like I was dragged here against my will."

He moved to take the seat next to mine, setting his red cup on the table between us. I glanced at the light blue polo he'd worn and the jeans I'd noticed fit him very well around the backside. His hair was done, and he looked a lot like he had back in seventh grade. Even better.

"I see you're enjoying a nice beverage of *agua* tonight." He motioned to the bottle sitting on my lap.

"And you're partaking in the libations of alcohol freely given at this party?" I gave him a small smile, emphasizing my sarcasm.

His smile grew even wider, and I frowned, trying to figure out what was so amusing about underage drinking. "Actually, I poured myself a soda. No alcohol. Not since…the accident." He turned his gaze away and took a sip from the cup, his jaw working back and forth. Was he trying not to cry?

"You mean you come to these parties and make people think you've been drinking when you really haven't?" The idea sounded both ludicrous and genius at the same time.

"My buddies know I don't drink anymore, but that's about it." His expression looked sad, his eyes glazed as if seeing something far away. "I was turning into my father, and the accident kind of woke me up a bit, helped me see that I didn't need all that. Besides, losing one of your best friends because he was driving your car doesn't help you sleep well at night as it is."

I wanted to come up with some retort to knock him down a peg, but this was a whole new side to Jake I hadn't seen before. There had been plenty of rumors swirling around after the accident saying that Jake had meant to get Troy Johnson killed. Others described how Troy had a fight with his girlfriend and Jake had jumped into the Jeep at the last minute, trying to dissuade him from driving away.

"I'm sorry, Jake. I didn't know." I leaned forward and reached my hand out, covering the back of his with my palm. Warmth trickled up my arm and into my chest, causing a feeling of comfort and giving me goosebumps.

"Well, it's just a piece of my life that's happened in the last three years, five months, and two days." It took a moment for me to realize what he meant with the numbers, but as I calculated it all, I realized it led to the day my mother walked out the door.

He swallowed. "That's the day my life started to crumble as well."

His eyes stared into mine as several emotions played out on his face. Most of them looked more vulnerable than anything, and I wanted to pull him toward me and play with his hair, telling him everything would be okay again. But something held me back, my pride most likely.

"Well, I'm here when you need to talk." I glanced at my phone, not sure I was ready for an in-depth conversation right there next to a pool at a loud party. Sure, I'd been looking for answers for so long, but now that I thought about it, did I really want to know? Even though my attraction toward him grew every time we were around each other, my subconscious seemed to know pursuing a relationship with him would be much harder than what I'd been doing before we started talking again.

I stood, playing with the lid of my water bottle as Jake stood before me.

"Where are you going?" he asked, his voice soft.

"I, uh…" I cleared my throat, trying to think of something. I glanced up and locked my eyes with his. "I should probably go find my friends, just to make sure they're okay, you know?"

Jake raised his arm past me and pointed through the window. "Serena, Brynn." I looked where he pointed and saw the two of them dancing with a couple of guys I didn't recognize. "Kate is probably still in the kitchen talking to the guy and girl she was chatting with when I asked where you were."

I shook my head, trying to process the words. "Wait, you asked her where I was?"

"I figured I'd give it a shot to see if you were here. I knew there would be at least one other sober person at this party, and I like spending time with you. It reminds me of the good old days." He ran his hand through his hair as if wishing he could take the statements back.

"Well, I promised them fifteen minutes, but I didn't think about what would happen after that amount of time. I rode with Kate." A sinking feeling took over. I was going to be stuck here all night. I didn't have a curfew, so that wasn't the issue. It was the boredom I was bound to feel once Jake found a girl to talk to.

"Why don't I drive you home? Then you won't be stuck here all night." He shrugged, the corner of his mouth turning up in a way that made me wonder if I was in a dream.

I must have stared at him a little too long because his smile disappeared and a frown replaced it. "You'd do that for me? What about your friends?" I asked.

"They'll be fine for a bit. I only drove Dax here. The others were just going to meet us here." Jake picked up his cup and motioned to the house. "Go tell Kate I'll give you a ride, and I'll let Dax know where I am."

My feet seemed to move on automatic, turning me in the direction of the house and walking right to Kate. I whispered in her ear so she could hear, and her grin was wider than I'd ever seen it.

I walked out the front door, grateful to be out in the fresh air and away from the thumping bass. Jake stepped onto the sidewalk from behind a bush, startling me a bit.

"Just me," he said, his hands out to reassure me. "I forgot how jumpy you get."

I chuckled at that comment, several memories playing through my head within about three seconds. "Yeah, I'm definitely not one to take through the haunted houses."

We walked down the sidewalk a ways, both of us quiet. For once, it felt like old times, where we could just let each other be and only talk when we needed to.

Jake opened the passenger door for me, and I nodded, grateful he was willing to take me home in the middle of a party. My heart raced as I waited for him to walk around the Jeep and get into the driver's seat. For some odd reason, this felt like a first date.

He started the engine and pulled out of the spot, turning around in the crowded cul-de-sac. "You look amazing, by the way. How does it feel to survive your first party?" He glanced over at me with a mischievous grin before turning his eyes back to the road. I was grateful for that small action as I felt safer when he was watching the road, and my breathing was able to get back to normal. His first words echoed in my mind, and I wanted to ask him more about it. But part of me was worried I wouldn't like the reasoning behind his flirty comment.

"That wasn't my first party. I went to one in ninth grade. It wasn't quite as loud and busy as this one, but it wasn't too bad."

"Ninth grade, huh," Jake asked, his wrist on top of the steering wheel and his other hand resting on the console between us. "That surprises me. You've always been straight-laced."

I turned a bit to face him, ready for whatever argument was about to ensue. "You were the same way, I remember. Was that just because of me or because that's who you were before this persona took over?"

When his face fell, I backpedaled, resting my hand on his forearm. "Jake, I didn't mean it like that. I know there's been a lot going on in your life. I guess I've just been jealous all this time that you didn't want to share it with me. That high school and popularity and girls could so easily replace what we'd had together."

He bit his lower lip, looking as though he was debating internally what he should say. "That's where you've got it wrong, Pen. It was never easy."

CHAPTER 19

JAKE

$\mathcal{A}$ storm of emotions swelled up within me, and I couldn't decide if I should explode or just do the best I could to calm them all down. Maybe taking Penny home was a mistake. I'd wanted to be with her, hear her talk a bit more, but somehow she just kept acting like I'd cast her off like an old worn-out shoe. Which I had done.

"My dad took the job promotion about two months before your mother walked out. You remember it, right? He invited your family over for that big cookout to celebrate."

I glanced at Penny, and she nodded slowly. "I'd forgotten about that. We ate three ice cream bars and swore we were going to be sick forever." She laughed, the sound of it easing some of the tension in the pit of my stomach.

"Right. I didn't realize the promotion would make it so he had to travel so often. He'd done a couple of trips a year before, but this was Monday to Friday stuff. At first, it was kind of nice because he didn't have a chance to ask me about baseball every time I was around him. But it was like he saved up every conversation for the weekend. It got to the point where I was starting to dislike baseball, just because he kept pushing it on me so much."

Penny's hand twitched, and I realized it was still on my forearm. The feeling was comforting and almost intimate.

"I remember having to drag you out a few times to play catch. I kept wondering what was wrong with you since it had been what we'd done for so many years." I glanced over, and it was as though a little light bulb had lit in her eyes.

I nodded, remembering how her eyes had been so fiery every time, telling me I would turn into a no-good worthless kid if I didn't stick with it. The passion of thirteen-year-olds.

"A couple weeks before your mom left, my dad came home drunker than I'd ever seen him. I woke up to him yelling at my mother, throwing her into walls and punching her in the face. I did my best to intervene, but he hit me in the stomach, taking all the air with it. I crumpled to the floor, trying to breathe, and he just stood above me, laughing." I cringed, remembering the details as vividly as the day it happened. "He leaned over and spit in my face, calling me a disappointment and a waste."

"Oh, Jake, I had no idea. Why didn't you tell me? I just thought you were being ornery because you were a teenager. I didn't know all that was happening."

I shrugged, turning the Jeep onto the main street once the stoplight turned green. "I think some part of me thought that if I couldn't protect my own mother from him, how could I protect anyone, ever?"

The words tasted acidic on my tongue, and saying them seemed to put everything into a clear movie reel. I'd started pulling away from Penny but hadn't quite understood at the time why. She'd been my rock for so long that it was difficult to drift away, find new friends or create stronger friendships with the ones I had. But I'd put up the walls to keep it from affecting me when I saw her outside looking like she'd lost her dog. And I'd kept telling myself she was better off without me.

"You were thirteen, and it's not like your dad is some small guy." The concern on her face as we pulled into her driveway helped with some of the bitter memories that sprang up again.

"I know, but at that age, you just think you're so big, you know? That you should be able to take care of your loved ones. But I failed my mom. And then it became a routine. He'd come home from a business trip, sloshed, and the fists would start flying. I made sure the twins stayed hidden as much as possible and did what I could to soften the blows for my mom, but she'd always end up with a black eye or a broken bone." I blew out a breath, trying to keep the anxiety of the memories from causing an attack. "I tried to report it several times, but my mother always smoothed it over, claiming it was her own clumsiness that caused each accident."

I paused a moment, feeling some relief as the words lifted a burden I'd been carrying for so long. I'd never mentioned anything to the guys, only saying we couldn't hang out at my house when my dad would be home. Finally breaking my silence made things clearer.

"Does he still do that?" Tears were in her eyes, and one slid down the side of her cheek, black trailing it from her mascara.

"Not as much anymore. He's moved on to other vices." I looked out the window and over at my house, seeing my mother's light on. My heart broke for her, but as much as she'd tried to get out, something always kept her there, taking the brunt of the blows, whether physical or emotional. It was probably me and my two sisters.

Penny placed her hands on my cheeks, turning my face toward her. Tears streaked down her face. "I'm the worst person in the world. After all this time, I thought you were the biggest jerk ever. But you were just trying to keep your family together as best as you could at thirteen and fourteen. I'm so sorry. I wish I'd been able to help."

Her words caused my own tears to surge. Why hadn't I trusted her with this before? I might have had someone to lean on, might not have lost Troy. Might have convinced my mother to move on and start a new life out of this cycle of nightmares.

With the Jeep in park, I reached over, wrapping my arm around her and pulling her to my chest as much as I could over the console in between us. She sobbed against me for several minutes, and a new sensation took over. I'd never really seen Penny cry, but to hold her and comfort her seemed like the most natural thing to do.

I stroked her hair, loving the feeling of the softness between my fingers. "Hey, it's okay. You shouldn't be the one crying. I'm the one who pushed you away."

Penny sat up, wiping under her eyes with her fingers. "But I should have kept pushing back. I should have known you had something more than just getting older that was making you act all weird."

She sniffed, and another stray tear started to fall. Reaching out, I wiped it away, my hand next to her lips, drawing my eyes to them. I'd thought about those lips more in the past few weeks than I'd thought about any lips in all my life.

I glanced up, watching her eyes as they searched my face for something. Pausing a second, I took a breath and moved in, brushing my lips to hers.

She stilled, and I pulled back, hoping I hadn't ruined

everything more than I'd already done before. Her gaze dipped back to my lips, and I leaned in again, this time wrapping my hand through her hair and around her neck, pulling her closer to intensify the kiss.

The warmth that flowed between us, as well as the sparks I could have sworn were going off, made me wonder how I could've ever thought about kissing another girl. Not that I'd ever kissed Penny before, but this moment was everything and more. It was like the world was finally righting itself, helping me get back to the vision of how my life was supposed to be.

A ringtone pierced the silence in the Jeep, and we both jumped back, looking as though we'd just been caught. I glanced down to see the screen of her phone on her lap. It was her father.

"You might want to answer that," I said, scooting back in my seat and running my hands through my hair.

"Uh, hey, Dad. Yeah, I got a ride home. I'll be right in." Penny hung up the phone, her eyes darting around to everything in the vehicle but my face. "I, um, I need to go. Thank you for the ride and for telling me all that. I'm not sure how you managed to keep all that bottled up for so long, but just know that I'm right next door. Call me or whatever, and we can talk if you need to."

Her hand squeezed mine, and she leaned forward, kissing me lightly on the cheek. She hesitated a moment before waving and getting out of the Jeep.

I leaned my head back against the headrest as I watched to make sure she made it inside. I wasn't sure how I'd gone from enemy number one to kissing her, but the bridge had been rebuilt, and I finally felt like my life wasn't a constant rollercoaster of emotions. Maybe I had a chance at a happily ever after despite what had happened before.

I glanced up as the light turned on in her window and Penny peeked out. I'd be lucky to have her by my side for the rest of my life. Now I just needed to make sure I didn't screw it up.

CHAPTER 20

PENNY

I was still thinking about that kiss on Thursday, days later. Even my lips seemed to have the humming feel of the vibrations imprinted on them, able to be called up at the slightest thought of a kiss. We'd had several games, and I had some tests to study for, so I hadn't been on the schedule for work since the week before, meaning I only got to see Jake in passing.

But every time my phone pinged, I'd race to see who the message was from. Jake had messaged me several times, and I might have gone back and looked at the conversations at least twenty times, analyzing them for the littlest details. Each time I'd bounce from disbelief to elation as I thought about all of our interactions over the past few weeks.

We hadn't even messaged about the kiss, or anything significant, for that matter. Had the kiss been because what he'd revealed to me was so secret? The thought made me cringe. I didn't want to be another girl on his list of conquests.

I arrived at school earlier than usual and took a seat on the large platform in the common area. Only a few people milled about at that time of the morning, and I pulled out a book, knowing I needed to finish it since the night would be taken up by a game forty-five minutes away.

"What's with the sad face, friend?" Kate slid up next to me and gave me a look of concern. "I would think you'd still be on cloud nine from this weekend."

I'd told Kate the whole story of Jake offering to drive me home and the breathtaking kiss when I'd seen her Saturday morning—minus Jake's confession—practically bouncing as I paced back and forth in my bedroom. But was I jumping to the conclusion that a kiss could mean something more, especially given Jake's reputation?

It had been my first kiss and an amazing one at that, but I had nothing to compare it to. Maybe I had been awkward and Jake was just being polite by not saying anything.

"Just trying to get this book read for English tomorrow. How are things with you? No sign of mystery kisser, huh?" I gave her a mischievous smile and bumped her shoulder with mine. Kate had told me a story of her own. Some guy had come into the party wearing a mask and had kissed her and then disappeared, leaving her with a mystery she was still trying to solve.

"I feel bad judging all the people in Superman movies. Like, you can't tell who that is? My brain was whirling so much that I barely remember any of his features. Although, I didn't mind his lips on mine."

I shook my head, laughing. "Who'd have thought we'd both get our first kiss on the same night? I'm just glad mine didn't happen at the party."

"Parties aren't so bad, Pen. It's just what you make of it, I guess. Maybe someday I'll know who my mystery kisser was."

The bell rang, and I shuffled to my class, not ready for the usual early morning motivational pop quiz my professor tended to give.

"Hey," I heard behind me but didn't turn, thinking it was for someone else. The voice said it again, this time with a hand on my shoulder. I turned to see Jake giving me a small smile.

"Hey. How have things been?" I asked, debating between being late to class and having a normal face-to-face conversation with him.

He played with his hair a moment before looking back at me. "Good. It's been good. I better not keep you from class. I know how you like being on time."

My insides were warring about the need to be prompt and kicking myself for even worrying about stuff like that.

"Text me later. We'll be on the bus around noon to head out to Westchester." I bit my lip, surprised I'd been so forward. Despite our history, it still felt like we were beginning all over again, and I hoped I hadn't gone too far.

Jake's face brightened, and he nodded. "Will do. That will help me get through my last class of the day. Too bad we don't have a game too."

I took a few steps backward and gave him a little wave. Part of the way down the hall were stairs, and I had to turn so I didn't stumble over them. I glanced back once more to see Jake in the same spot, looking as gorgeous as a Greek statue.

I was heading for real trouble when it came to him. I just hoped his change of heart lasted longer than a couple of weeks.

CHAPTER 21

JAKE

"Are you guys dating or not? You've never had such a problem deciding before, Jake." Dax opened a protein bar and sat down on the bench between the lockers in the guys' locker room. He took a large bite, his lips smacking so loudly I had to turn away to keep from gagging.

"We haven't talked about that. It was just one kiss, Dax. I don't know if she wants to date me after all I've done to her." I sat on the bench, untying the laces on my sneakers. It was nice that we were the only ones in the locker room. I'd have been mortified if any of the other guys at the school heard me trying to figure out where I stood with a girl.

Dax finally swallowed and said, "She kissed you back. I'd say there's definitely potential there."

For the hundredth time, I thought about the kiss I'd shared with Penny, and with the way my lips still tingled at the thought, I wondered if she felt the same. Seeing her in the hall that morning had been awkward at first, but when she'd said to text her, something like hope exploded within me.

"But the kiss came after me talking about my dad's alcohol problem. You don't think she just felt bad for me?" I'd finally confided in Dax about my home situation the day before, knowing he wouldn't say anything to the other guys. I didn't need it going around school that things were complicated outside of baseball.

Dax stopped to think. "I've never seen you analyze a relationship as much as this one. That means you've got it bad for her, man." He took another bite of his bar and chewed a couple of times before saying, "Sometimes a kiss is just a kiss, you know."

That didn't reassure me at all. I opened the messaging app on my phone and scrolled through the short messages we'd sent each other over last period. The final one said her team made it to the school where the game was to be played, so I had to settle for radio silence for the next several hours. At least I had baseball practice to keep me occupied for some of it.

A bunch of other guys came in and started dressing. The sound of lockers squeaking open and jokes being passed back and forth broke the silence I'd had just moments before.

"Listen up," came Coach Maddox's voice from somewhere in the room. "We're going to have some college coaches at our game tomorrow, so I suggest you all work out the kinks today. These are some big schools, and the opportunity to attend would be worth your effort."

I had peeked around the lockers, and he glanced my way, nodding as if to single me out silently. Play baseball in college? I'd just now begun to like baseball again, as my father had eased up on it quite a bit, but would I still love it if I had to play and practice all the time at a more competitive level?

Maybe it was worth a shot, worth just doing the best I could tomorrow and seeing what happened from there. The least I could do was try, and if I decided I didn't want to play baseball after high school, I'd just tell them no.

I tapped out a message to Penny, knowing she wouldn't get it for a while but still wanting to send it anyway.

Coach said some college coaches will be at the game tomorrow.

I paused and tried to think of something else to say. Instead of putting any other emotions down, I pressed send and tucked the phone away in my backpack in my locker. Penny would know what to say, and I hoped she'd respond by the time we were done with practice.

CHAPTER 22

PENNY

e all got on the bus as the sun had almost set, ready for the long drive back home. I'd had an awesome day both on the mound and at the plate, and I felt like I was on top of the world.

"Great game today, ladies," Coach Ambrose said.

As she took her seat at the front of the bus, we all settled in. I pulled out my phone and stuck in my earbuds, knowing I needed to make the most of the ride back home. I looked for my music and saw I'd received a message from Jake three hours earlier.

Coach said some college coaches will be at the game tomorrow.

It was such a vague statement, and I wondered how he felt about it.

That's a good thing, right? You'll be able to show off your skills and get a scholarship for it.

I pressed send, staring at the screen as if his response would appear because I willed it. After nearly a minute with no answer, I started my music and continued reading Hamlet, going through it slowly so I could understand the older language and make sure I got the story correct. I loved

English, but Shakespeare seemed to be my own kind of torture just to keep my grades up.

The message pinged in my ears, and I turned the screen on and saw a message from Jake.

I guess. I'm not sure about it yet. I had a rough day at practice. I might not have anything to show them.

The defeatist attitude was something I hated, but after everything he'd talked about on Saturday, I could understand it. He'd probably gotten so sick of his dad badgering him about his practicing and skills that he either didn't think he was really good enough or he didn't want to go to college and see his father gloat.

You'll be fine. I'll come watch after we get done with our practice tomorrow. Just play like you always do. A cocky, arrogant shortstop who's better than everyone out there.

I don't play like that. Usually I'm just hoping I don't screw anything up.

I bit my lip as I read through his words. A wide smile took over, and I typed out, *You fooled me then.*

Several minutes went by, and I was worried I'd offended him. But then a long bubble popped up, and I realized what had taken so long.

At least I fooled someone. Tomorrow's a big game, and I hope we do well. My stomach is already twisted in knots. Sorry, I shouldn't bug you while you're on the bus.

Please, you're helping me avoid my reading for tomorrow.

I waited again and had to click the screen to keep it from going black.

What about you and college? Have you had any interest so far?

I'd gotten mail from at least fifty of the smaller schools, but after checking the classes and majors they offered, I'd been able to narrow it down to ten from there. I still would've preferred some of the bigger schools, but it was still early, and I had another year before graduation.

A few. I'll have a better chance of being looked at over the summer.

I'm at the diner tonight. Wish you were here.

I read the last phrase at least a dozen times, my chest nearly bursting with excitement.

Me too.

I sent it, not wanting to say too much or too little. I liked this simple relationship, where we were slowly feeling things out. From everything I'd learned over the past few years, this was different than any relationship Jake had had with other girls. Usually, they started and ended within a week. It was nearing a week since the kiss, and we'd barely seen each other. Was that the secret to a longer relationship with Rosemont's playboy?

He didn't text me back, and I knew he was probably swamped with the dinner crowd at the diner. I stared out the window for a while, imagining several scenarios of the next time I saw him before turning back to my book. If I got it done now, I might be able to see him once I got home and before bed.

I never would have thought I'd want to get my homework done so I could see a boy. Especially not Jake White.

CHAPTER 23

JAKE

I pulled into my driveway after a long shift at the diner. Glancing over, I saw Penny's car in the drive, and I looked up at her window, wondering if she was already asleep or not. We were different in that way. I was a night owl and usually didn't go to sleep until after midnight, no matter the day. Penny, on the other hand, seemed to clock out by at least ten unless she was studying for something.

Opening the door, I stepped out of the Jeep and walked toward the side door of my house.

"Hey, long night at work?" Penny's voice came from the side, causing me to jump for once.

She giggled, and I shook my head.

"I can't believe you got me. It's been forever since someone scared me like that."

Penny stepped out of the bush and grinned. "I thought I'd give it a try. You look tired."

"Claudia was in a mood today, so I had to work double-time to make sure she didn't end up throwing plates against the wall again. Lou laughed every time I came back with another load of dishes, and the place was packed until about thirty minutes ago." I leaned against the Jeep and folded my arms, taking in her appearance.

Her auburn hair shone a bit in the moonlight, and it was all down, looking a little damp still. She wore bright pink and purple heart pajama bottoms and a plain gray t-shirt.

"How was your game?" I asked, watching the features of her face turn into a smile.

Penny moved over to lean next to me on the Jeep. "It was really good. Seventeen strikeouts and three really good hits."

"Oh man! I would've been so bored out in the field with seventeen strikeouts. Sounds like you were on fire, though."

She nodded. "It felt good. Coach Ambrose was really happy too. I think I'm warming up to her."

Her hair tickled my arm, and I lifted my hand to rub the spot. A few seconds later, she leaned her head against my shoulder, and I froze, unsure what to do. This had never happened to me, where I wasn't Mr. Casanova with a girl. But this was Penny Davis, my oldest friend and next-door neighbor. If I screwed this up, it would end up being worse than anything before.

Unfolding my arm, I draped it around her shoulders and pulled her in a bit. "What do you mean 'warming up to her'? Coach Maddox said she's always raving about you."

Penny leaned back, her eyebrows pinched together. "I've never heard that. I think today was the second time she's told me good job since the season started. But maybe that's good for me so I keep pushing myself." She sighed, laying her head against me again.

"That could be a good reason," I said, wondering if she could hear my heart thudding around in my chest with her ear right next to it. "I should probably head in. I've got some homework to finish up, and then I need to sleep for the game tomorrow."

Penny jumped away from me and waved her pointer

finger at my face. "Who are you, and what have you done with Jake White? The Jake I know hardly ever does his homework."

Raising my hands as if she were pointing a gun at me, I laughed. "Well, someone has been telling me to step up my game and take advantage of the skills and talents I have. I figured I won't make it far or even to a decent college if I don't make some kind of an effort." I winked at her and then tapped the tip of her nose with my finger.

"So you're actually thinking about college now? That's awesome, Jake. You'll be amazing. Did your coach tell you which college coaches will be at the game tomorrow?"

I shook my head. "No, just made a point to give me a long stare. He's been telling me to think about it for the last few weeks. We'll see how it goes tomorrow."

Penny reached forward and rested her hand on my forearm. "Please. Just fool everyone with your amazing diving skills and the most accurate swing I've ever seen, and the coaches will be lining up at your door."

Heat rushed to my cheeks, surprising me that a compliment could make me feel so embarrassed. I'd received plenty of praise over the last several years, but for some reason, Penny's words hit home. Probably because from the look on her face, they were the most genuine of any I'd heard before.

I reached out for her and wrapped my arms around her back, pulling her to my chest. She wrapped her arms around my waist, the top of her head resting just under my chin. I held on to her for longer than was probably acceptable, but something about it infused more confidence in me, like someone else really cared about what I did with my life. If only things could stay this simple.

"Good luck tomorrow," Penny said, pulling away a few inches. She stretched up on her tiptoes and kissed my cheek, leaving the spot tingling. Giving me a quick smile, she turned toward her house.

"Don't screw this up, Jake," I whispered to myself. If I just took it slow, hopefully I wouldn't mess up the greatest thing I had going for me at the moment.

* * *

"WHAT ARE you doing home so late?" roared my father.

I took a step back, surprised to see him home on a Thursday night. Usually, his work kept him out of town until Friday afternoon.

I frowned, bending over to take off my shoes by the door and hang up my bag on the hooks. Keeping things orderly helped my mom's anxiety stay at a minimum, and it was the least I could do when I came inside.

"Answer me, son!" His large figure towered above me as he grabbed my arm, but as I stood to face him, a flicker of fear passed over his face. He hadn't been around much in the last few months, and I was now just an inch or two shorter than he was. He had at least fifty pounds on me, but if needed, I'd employ my speed and run away from him if the conversation escalated.

"I was at the diner, paying my debt to society, all right?" I knocked his hand away from my arm and walked past, feeling more confident than I had in past years.

His heavy footsteps thundered behind me. "Don't walk away when I'm talking to you. I'm still your father."

Whirling around, I stopped short, causing him to go off-balance. His arms flailed to the side, and the smell of his breath reeked of alcohol.

"Where are your mother and the girls? I've been here over an hour, and no one has picked up my calls." He staggered over to sit in the recliner in the family room, leaning back with his legs propped up.

"I don't know, Dad. I can't have my phone out at work. Like I said, I just got home. If you don't need anything else, I need to go shower. I smell like dirt and grease."

"How's baseball going? I talked to your coach on the phone yesterday, and he said you've got some college coaches coming to watch the game tomorrow. I came home early so I could watch it."

With just a few words, the excitement and confidence I'd felt with Penny plummeted to the ground. Every time my father showed up to one of my games, it only ended in disaster, with him yelling at everything and everyone on the field.

I shook my head. "You really didn't have to do that, Dad. I doubt any of them will be there for me."

"Nonsense. You've always had the talent to succeed more than anyone I know. I haven't been to any of your games in a while, so this will be good. I could even go undercover and chat up some of the coaches, see what they think, you know?"

I groaned. "Please don't do that, Dad. If there's even a chance of me playing baseball in college, just let me prove it to them on the field. Please." I hated hearing the begging in my voice, but at least twelve different scenarios had played out in my mind since he'd suggested it seconds before, and I felt sick at the prospect of even one of them coming true.

"Too good for your dad now, huh? Don't worry. I'll just stay to myself."

I took in a deep breath, not feeling the boldness I'd held on to when I first got inside the door. As much as I wanted to plead with him not to come to the game, I knew it would only anger him into coming for sure.

"No, Dad. Just let me take care of it during the game, okay? Next year, if I don't have any prospects still, I'll let you talk to some of the recruiters." A silent plea went up that I would have a few offers by then. Because if I was going to play in college, I didn't want to be embarrassed by him trying to "work things" and screwing it all up.

He slapped the arm of the recliner and grinned, the glazed look in his eyes making him look a little insane. "I'm just glad you're coming around to the idea of getting a scholarship. You've got the talent to go far, and I thought I was going to have to beat some sense into you sooner or later. Now I don't have to." Picking up the remote, he flipped the TV on and scrolled through the guide.

I blew out a breath and ran upstairs, the adrenaline of his words now echoing through me like a vibration of my anger from his words.

Did I fake being sick tomorrow? The thought barely entered my mind when I shrugged it off.

I could get through this. I'd been through much worse, and with Penny there, cheering me on, I was bound to have a decent game. I just hoped my dad would keep to himself like he promised.

CHAPTER 24

PENNY

*P*ractice went longer than usual, and I grabbed my bag and ran in the direction of the baseball field, not even taking time to remove my cleats. I sat on the side of the third baseline and removed them, all the while trying to catch up on what had happened during the game. The Rosemont Royals were down by four runs, and at that moment, Jake was stepping into the batter's box.

I stuffed my cleats into the bag and stepped into my slip-ons before standing up next to the fence and yelling, "You've got this, Jake!"

He was usually so laser-focused, but he glanced over in my direction as he set his feet, a fleeting smile on his face. He took the first pitch, a ball on the outside corner.

I stuffed my bag next to some of the bags already there and ran up the bleachers. It was difficult to find a seat since so many had come out to the cross-town rivalry game.

I slipped in next to Kate and a few of her officer people and watched as Jake swung and missed at a curveball that moved so far out of the zone he didn't have a chance of hitting it.

"Come on, Jake! You're better than that!" I heard a familiar voice bellow from behind me, and I knew part of the story. It was Jake's dad. No wonder he was so tense.

I cupped my hands over my mouth, hoping he could hear me from the batter's box. "You can hit this guy, Jake. Find your pitch. Wait for your pitch."

The pitcher from the opposing team wound up and threw the ball to home plate, the fastball coming on the inside corner and nearly hitting Jake in the hands. He spun out and missed the impact, but the crowd booed, not happy about the near-miss on injuring one of our best players.

I wrung my hands together, trying to send any good vibes I could his way as I heard his father grumbling from the bench a few rows up.

The pitch came in, and Jake drove it into a gap in the outfield, driving in a run as he made it to second base. I stood and clapped, whistling as loud as I could. Second base didn't make for the easiest view, but I saw a glint of a smile on his face before he turned it back to a somber expression as his teammate stepped into the box.

"So, have you finally changed your mind about liking him?" Kate asked when I sat down again.

Heat traveled all the way to the tips of my ears. "Maybe."

"It's about time. I was beginning to think I was going to have to stage some kind of intervention or something to get you to see how that boy is head over heels for you. And I'm pretty sure you feel the same."

I didn't say anything, only stared out at the attractive guy on second base, wondering if he really felt the same.

The game progressed, and the boys were slowly coming back, but the other team was doing a good job of keeping the Royals on their toes.

When the game finally ended with Rosemont losing by one point, I could see the defeat in the slump of Jake's shoulders. But he'd played his heart out, and while that wasn't enough to make up for the early deficit, I knew whatever college recruiters had been there would've seen that over the win.

I waited for the crowds to leave, and a bunch of us students waited for the coach's pep talk in the outfield to be over before the players started gathering up equipment to head back into the locker room.

"They did so well; don't you think?" Kate asked, looping her arm through mine. "I know they lost, but at least they didn't get killed."

"I guess that's one way to look at it." Any loss was hard to swallow, especially if the end goal was to make it to the state championship, but I needed to hold onto Kate's positivity when I got the chance to talk to Jake in a few minutes.

Kate tugged on my arm. "That guy looks really familiar." She pointed to Dax, the catcher, and I shrugged.

"He's been the team's catcher for a while. You've probably just seen him hanging out with Jake in the halls."

"What if he's my mystery kisser?" Kate asked, eyes wide with excitement.

Sighing, I shook my head. "Are you still trying to solve that mystery? I don't know if you'd want Dax to be the one to fit your man. He's just as much of a ladies' man as the rest of them."

"Well, look at Jake. He's a good example of a reformer. I haven't heard anything about him hanging out with any other ladies ever since you two have been talking again."

The thought of it put my mind at ease. If anyone were to hear of anything, it would be Kate. But that still didn't make it one hundred percent fail-proof, and I did my best to hide my momentary excitement.

"It's been maybe a month since we started talking. I don't know if reformed is a word I would use yet. But he's been sweet to me." I searched for Jake amid the boys who'd come out of the dugout as they threw cleats and gloves into their bat bags.

Feeling anxious for him, I walked over to the end of the cinderblock dugout and rounded the corner. Jake stood stock-still in front of his father, his features tight and his lips pulled into a line.

"I don't know if you'll get any offers after the way you played today, Jake. You looked like an absolute idiot when you swung and missed at that curveball. Grab your things. We're going to go practice again at home." I watched as Mr. White grabbed Jake's upper arm, pushing him toward the dugout.

"Dad, I've got to work at the diner again."

I shook my head, knowing he hadn't been scheduled for that night, and Jake's gaze drifted in my direction, his eyes going wide as if trying to tell me something.

His father's phone rang, and he turned to answer it. In that time, Jake shook his head, looking terrified.

"Don't let him see you. I'll talk to you later," he said, looking like he was going to be sick.

I took a few steps back, glancing at his father's back. It was tempting to stay and give Dave White a piece of my mind after everything Jake had told me. But it seemed like now wasn't the time.

"Just remember how awesome you are," I said just loud enough for him to hear before I turned and made my way back to Kate.

"What happened? Did you get to talk to him?" Kate looked more confused than ever and pointed in the direction Jake was standing.

I grabbed her arm and pulled her along behind me. "I think Jake and his dad are having a little argument. I need to grab my bag."

"Okay, well, some of us are meeting at the ice cream shop in about thirty minutes. Brynn, Hazel, and Serena are going to meet us there. You coming?"

I jogged to grab my bag and ran back to her, grateful Jake's dad was still on the phone. "Let me see what's going on at home, and I'll let you know."

What I really wanted to do was make sure Jake would be okay, that he had some out if he needed it. My dad liked the fact that I pushed myself to practice as much as I did, but after a long game, more practice wasn't going to help.

"Sounds good. Text me when you're on your way."

* * *

I HUNG out in the parking lot for another twenty minutes, waiting for Jake and his dad to appear from the field. At one point, I even walked down far enough to see his dad throwing pitches to him from behind a screen.

No wonder Jake had begun to hate baseball.

After several more pitches, they picked up the balls and packed up.

I ran back to my car and drove it up next to Jake's Jeep so I'd have a chance to talk to him, hopefully alone.

Jake walked into the locker room, and his dad continued on to his car. When I saw him pull out on to the main road, I breathed a sigh of relief. I don't know what I expected, maybe that his dad would start beating him right there if I didn't stick around to help.

Ten minutes later, Jake emerged from the school, rubbing his wet hair as he walked out to his car.

I opened my door and stepped out, taking in the look of frustration on his face. "Hey," I said, leaning on my car.

"Hey." It was short and clipped, the tone bothering me a bit. How selfish was I? The guy had just been ripped to shreds by his father, and I was worrying about how he was reacting?

"I think you did pretty well out there. That one play you made, diving to get the guy out at—"

"Not now, Pen." He put out his hand in a stopping motion and then raised it to rub at the sides of his forehead.

I hesitated, unsure of how to help him. I'd never seen this side of Jake, the broken spirit and looking so tired. Taking a step forward, I wrapped my arms around his waist from the back as he loaded his bag into the back of the Jeep.

"I'm here when you need me, okay?" I mumbled into his back.

He slammed the door shut and turned slowly in my embrace, his arms warm around my neck. "Thanks. I'm going to head out."

"Go home? What about your dad? You told him you had to work."

Jake released his grip on me and shook his head. "Dad called Lou and asked. Because I lied, I had to do more batting practice right then." He looked like he was near tears then, and I pulled his face toward mine, resting my forehead on his.

"You've got me. Just know that I care about you, no matter how you play on the field. Come with me to the ice cream shop. At least that will help you avoid him for a little bit." I searched his face, looking for any emotion that might help me know how to comfort him. But it was a smooth mask at the moment, and I wasn't prepared with a Jake manual that addressed this kind of mood.

He finally nodded. "Okay. I'll meet you there."

Stepping away, he started the car and took off, leaving me in a cloud of black smoke.

I was torn. How was I supposed to help him when I didn't

completely understand what he was going through? Did I just make myself available to listen when he needed it?

Never had I longed more for the simpler days before our lives had been upturned. It was going to take longer than I thought to get back there, but I knew it would be worth it. At least, I hoped it was.

CHAPTER 25

JAKE

I had no desire to socialize with anyone at that point, but anything was better than heading back home. Mental and physical exhaustion took over, and a measure of humiliation flooded through me as I wondered who else had seen the scene my dad had made.

Penny waiting for me in the parking lot was one of the last things I wanted, and I hoped she hadn't heard any of what my dad said. After each ball I'd hit, he'd spout off some critique, usually ending it with a few colorful words and some insult to my skills. I'd started to love baseball again, but if this was how my life would be for the next year and a half until I graduated, I wasn't sure I even wanted to stay on the team. But then again, what would I have to look forward to every day? At least my dad was gone during the week.

But when Penny hugged me, telling me that her being there was not based on my performance on the field, it felt more like home than my physical house did. And as much as I didn't want to interact with anyone else at the moment, I needed more assurance that I could be just another teen out with friends. Besides, I had no intention of seeing my father in the next few hours, and staying away from him was the best way to accomplish that.

The group was big when I got to the ice cream shop. It was actually a good thing as I didn't have all the attention on me like it usually was, to provide some kind of entertainment or commentary.

Penny sat next to me, her hand on mine under the table, and I was grateful for her presence. If anything, reconnecting with her had made a huge difference over the past month. If only I could shield her from the fury of my father.

"What's wrong with you, man?" Colt asked, punching me in the right shoulder.

"Long day, man. Just need to chill for a bit. What brought you guys here?" I looked behind him and saw Dax, Ben, and Nate. Dax's eyes dipped down to Penny's hand on mine, and he grinned. I pulled it away and scratched the crown of my head, avoiding Penny's gaze and hoping she would understand why I did it.

I slid out of the booth to greet them with our random handshakes, and several of the people at the tables around, all from the same group, were watching us with an intensity I wasn't in the mood for.

"We heard a bunch of people were coming here. We didn't expect to see you here, though, especially after the conversation with your dad." Dax's eyes narrowed.

My stomach sank, and I looked at my shoes like I was inspecting something. I wished he wasn't able to read me so easily. He reminded me of Troy, and while I needed someone like that in my life, I wished they didn't see everything when I didn't want them to.

"You can all join us," Kate said from behind Penny.

Dax's eyes flicked to her and went wide. He turned and pretended to inspect the menu. I'd have to ask him what was going on there later.

I glanced back at Penny and Kate, seeing Penny's hooded eyes.

"We're good," Ben said, giving a short wave. "I think we're going to head out to the new movie at the theater." He gripped the shoulders of Nate and Colt, his grin more of a demand than a question.

"Okay, good luck. I'll see you at school tomorrow," I murmured as they waved on their way to the door.

Dax grabbed a cone and headed out behind the guys, taking a look back at Kate before leaving the ice cream shop. There was definitely something there, and it relieved something inside of me. Kate seemed like a nice girl, totally opposite from the girls Dax usually went for. Maybe she'd be good for him in the long run.

I slid back into the booth next to Penny and moved my hand over to her leg. Her elbows were on the table, her hands cradling her head as she listened to a conversation going on across the table. She didn't look my way at all, and I knew it was my fault. I wasn't used to having a girlfriend for long amounts of time, but is that what we were? Boyfriend and girlfriend? Or were we just slowly getting back to the friend stage?

I reflected on our kiss, knowing that was way more intense than what friends would feel. Time. That's what we needed: more time. I'd just have to talk to her and tell her that maybe if we took things slow, we'd have a chance of something more than just next-door neighbor best friends.

The group finished up their desserts, and a bunch of people talked about meeting up at someone's house for a movie.

I pulled Penny to the side. "I'm not really feeling like a movie right now, but I'd like to talk. Do you want to meet back at home, and we'll chat?"

She avoided my gaze, her lips pursed and arms folded

tightly against her chest. When she spoke, her voice was soft but tense. "If you're going to tell me you're no longer talking to me because of your friends, you might as well do it here."

"What are you talking about?" I asked, placing my hands on her upper arms. "I'm not going back to the jerk I was before, okay? I would just rather spend time as the two of us than a big group tonight. Come on. It's been a long day, and I could use that listening ear you claimed to have."

Her lips turned up at the corners, though hesitant, and she looked me in the eyes. "Okay, I'll meet you at home."

The whole drive I tried to think of what I wanted to talk about, hoping I could word things better than I usually did around Penny. I wanted to keep going in our relationship, but I had been dubbed the "playboy" or the "serial dater" for so long that I really didn't know how to make anything work long term.

I pulled into my driveway right after she pulled into hers. She stepped out, and I jogged to her in a few steps.

"Let's go out on the swing." I motioned behind me to my backyard. The swing was sitting underneath the small deck my father had built when I was eight or nine, the only thing my parents allowed to be out during the night.

Reaching for her hand, I enveloped it with my own. "Your hand is cold. Do you want me to go get a blanket?"

Penny shook her head. "No, I'll be fine. We just had ice cream, remember?"

I'd nearly forgotten that with my mind spinning on the way home.

Penny sat on the swing first, and I took a spot next to her. I wrapped my arm around her shoulders and pulled her closer to me, the comfort I'd felt during our earlier hug returning. The smell of vanilla from her hair seemed to relax me even more, and I stared out into the dark sky spotted with billions of stars.

She sighed, and I waited a bit longer, making sure I had what I wanted to say ready to go.

"I'm sorry about the ice cream shop, Pen. To be honest, I'm just that awkward and didn't know how to explain us holding hands to Dax."

Her head popped up, and she stared into my eyes, not believing it. "What do you mean you're awkward? Aren't you supposed to be some ladies' man?"

The comment stung a bit, but I knew she was right. "You mean a lot to me, Penny. More than any girl I've ever gone out with, and I just don't want to screw things up, you know? I've already done that once, and I know if it happens again, you won't be giving me another chance."

"You're right about that," she said, nodding. "So what do you want to do about it? Is this one of those 'define the relationship' talks I've heard so much about?"

The way she said it pulled a laugh right out of me, and I doubled over, trying to control myself. She punched me lightly, and I sat back, finally calming down.

"I'm sorry, but I think that was one of the best lines I've heard from you in a while." I wiped at a few tears that had escaped from my outburst and grinned at her. "Sure, I guess you could say this is a DTR moment. Would you want to date me, Penelope Davis?"

It was her turn to laugh, and she said, "I think if you can stop being an idiot, being your girlfriend would be good. But you can't just pretend we aren't together when your friends are around. Are you ashamed to be seen with me because I'm not some high school Barbie?"

Point taken. "I promise I'm not ashamed to be with you. And you are hotter than any Barbie I've ever seen." I paused, giving her a small smile. "I just don't want to hurt you. Ever again. But will you go easy on me for the first few weeks? I've never dated someone longer than a week, maybe two."

"So you're saying you want us to be together for three weeks?" One corner of her mouth lifted, and the smirk sent a shockwave of feeling through me. Most of the girls I'd dated in the past were all about the notoriety of hanging out with me, of kissing me, etc. Penny was different, and for the first time in my life, I realized I needed that.

I rolled my eyes and gave an exaggerated sigh. "Please. I want this to go on as long as it works for us."

I reached over and intertwined my fingers with hers, feeling the rush of heat and excitement flood to the rest of my body. Leaning over, I pressed my lips to hers, keeping the kiss simple but filled with promise.

In that moment, I felt like the awkward young teenager I was, but somehow I knew this was right. I'd been chasing cheap imitations of Penny for too long, and it was nice to finally be where we were. If I was going to make this work, I'd have to do the opposite of everything I usually did with other girls. But with her support, I might just survive high school.

CHAPTER 26

The next month passed like the blink of an eye with both Jake and I busy with baseball and softball, homework, and working at the diner. We often studied at each other's houses, sharing kisses here and there, which made me realize why everyone made such a big deal about relationships. There were always going to be challenges, but to have my best friend back was like a dream come true. And the fact that he was now my boyfriend? The preteen me would have been squealing for weeks at the thought.

It was interesting to see the changes in Jake too. He'd kept his word at taking things slow, and it was almost like our separation had never happened. He was also working harder and with more determination to reach his new goals for after high school than I'd seen before we started hanging out again. With grades higher and a few letters from schools to play baseball, he was finally getting more excited about the prospect of what could happen in the future.

He'd had a few run-ins with his father, but we'd talked about them for the most part. It was hard to see him so down about things when, in reality, his father had just skewed the facts, making it look as though Jake hadn't been improving or wasn't trying. But at least we'd managed to convince his dad we would practice together instead of him repeating the scene from that game with the college coaches.

It was April, and I was feeling the pressure as I studied for each of my advanced placement classes. I'd be taking the tests at the end of April, and as each day passed, my stomach tightened even further. Doubt came soon after. Would I be able to pass all the tests I had to take? What had I been thinking to take this heavy of a schedule?

Jake had been over at the beginning of the week, but we'd missed each other the past few nights, so the knock on the front door on Thursday evening didn't mean much to me.

Derrick came up to my room. "There's something at the door for you." He grinned, and I frowned. I didn't have money to order anything online, and it wasn't like people were constantly throwing gifts in my direction.

I threw on a hoodie and walked downstairs, grumbling about being interrupted while I was studying. Opening the door, I found several candles all over the porch with a giant blow-up baseball.

Poking my head out, I glanced around the dark yard, wondering what was happening.

"Why don't you actually read what it says on the ball, Penny?" Derrick's voice sounded annoyed.

My bare feet stepped onto the porch, and I pulled the ball toward me, seeing writing on it. The script was more feminine than anything.

Reading it out loud, I said, "'I might strike out asking, but will you be my catch at prom?'" Was this someone asking me to prom in two weeks? I'd been to a girl's-ask dance and had done a creative ask, but the guys had always just accepted it at school. This was new territory for me.

I turned to Derrick. "Did you see who did this? Was it

Jake?" We hadn't talked about the dance at all, and I wasn't even sure if he was up for things like that.

My brother shrugged and leaned against the wall. "I don't know. Maybe you should look around for the clues to the name. That's what most people do in these situations."

I poked him in the chest, laughing. "Oh yeah, Mr. I've-never-gone-on-a-date. What makes you the expert now?"

He raised his arms in defense. "I'm a good listener. Most of the girls will talk about it during classes when their older siblings have asked people to dances."

I looked around the porch, picking up a few of the flameless candles and checking the bottoms for clues. As I neared the end of the porch, my eyes adjusted somewhat to the darkness, and I saw several yellow balls littered around the yard.

"I think I found something. Come help me, Derrick."

Even though he sighed as if it was the last thing he wanted to do, he came out and gathered several balls, dropping them on the living room floor for me. I expected him to disappear back into his room like he'd done lately, but he seemed to hover, waiting for me to figure out my mystery date.

The back door opened, and I heard the familiar staccato of my father's steps coming through the kitchen. "I'm home. How was your— what happened here?"

"Penny got asked to prom. Now she just has to unscramble these letters."

"That's a lot of letters. Does the kid have four or five names?" My dad scratched the top of his head and chuckled, something he did when he thought his jokes were actually funny.

I shrugged. "I'm not sure yet. But we'll see, I guess."

I pulled all the balls together so the letters were visible. With all of them there, I searched for a J or a W but was confused when I didn't see one. I tried several combinations as I thought about boys from our school, but each one who was a potential decent date didn't work out.

As the letters came together, my heart dropped a bit. Nate Everton. I barely knew the friend of Jake's, only that he was a baseball player. Why would he ask me to the dance?

A mixture of sadness and confusion rushed through me.

"Who's Nate Everton?" my dad asked, eating a chip right after. The crunch of it was loud as he kept his mouth open with each bite.

"Ew, Dad. Close your mouth, please." I looked back at the letters. "A kid on the baseball team."

I turned back to see an amused expression on my dad's face. "So, what happened to Jake? Did he already ask you?"

"No," I said, looking at the name spelled out before me. We hadn't talked about going to the dance together, and we didn't have many classes in the same area, so I didn't see him often at school unless it was for baseball. Was he ashamed to go with me? As much as I tried not to, worries flashed before my eyes, and I focused on the last few times I'd been with Jake. Nothing had seemed off. Did I miss something?

"What are you going to do?" my dad asked, leaning against the doorframe.

Standing up, I walked over and stuck my foot into my slippers. "I'm going to go talk to Jake right now."

CHAPTER 27

JAKE

The guys had spent most of practice chatting about who they were going to ask to prom or how they were going to ask. At one point, I wanted to start chucking balls at them to get them to shut up.

Dances had never been my thing. I'd been asked several times to the girl's-ask dances, and up until the accident, I'd gone. But things had changed when Troy died the night we were coming home from prom the year before.

Now anything that involved getting dressed up reminded me of that night, and I hadn't been able to shake it. I avoided those nights as though I was quarantined in my room, because the rumors would start up again, and I didn't need to relive them through other people's words. I already did that enough when I tried to sleep.

I pulled out my math textbook, wishing I could somehow will the answers to appear on the page. It was the subject I was struggling with the most, but I needed to get it done. I was on a roll with all the changes I'd been making, and even my teachers had pointed it out. Maybe there was hope for me yet.

A knock came at my door, and I said, "Come in." I'd been trying to remember the formula we'd talked about in class, but it still didn't make sense after several minutes of reading through it.

"Penny's downstairs. Do you want me to send her up?" my mom asked, barely opening the door.

"Yeah. She might be able to help me figure this out."

A minute or two later, Penny walked in, her expression tight. Her lips were a thin line, and I could see the muscle along her jaw flexing.

"Hey, girl." I stood and walked over, leaning down to kiss her. Her lips were firmer than normal, not forming to mine quite so easily. "I didn't know you were coming over tonight. Don't you have a big test to study for?"

She folded her arms against her chest, and I could tell from the ramrod-straight way she stood that something was up.

"I was studying for a test when Derrick came and told me someone had left something at my door." Her eyebrows rose as if she were accusing me of telepathy.

"You got a package? What was in it?" I walked back to the chair at my desk, sitting in it sideways so I could face her.

She moved to sit on the edge of my bed, and I had to keep the grin off my face when I saw her giant puppy dog slippers.

"I got asked to prom, Jake. And it wasn't by you." Her voice warbled a bit at the end as if she was keeping everything together long enough to get the words out.

The air rushed out of my lungs, and from her body language and tone, I knew I was in trouble. If only I'd taken the time to talk to her about the whole thing, to explain that dances were PTSD-triggering situations for me. I searched her face, hoping to find the answer to what I needed to do to make things right.

When I saw her stony expression, I raised my hands.

"Okay, who asked you?" I tried to think of any guys who'd been interested in Penny at school but kept coming up blank.

"Nate."

"Nate Everton? No, he wouldn't ask you out. He knows we're together." I ran a hand through my hair, feeling like I'd just jumped onto an emotional rollercoaster. I wasn't as close to him as I was with Dax, but he wouldn't go behind my back like that, would he? Thinking over the conversations at practice earlier, he'd been more quiet than normal. Was this his chance to get back at me for throwing him through the window? He had been ready to ask Penny out that day.

Penny threw her hands into the air and stood, pacing back and forth in the room. "The evidence is in my front room, Jake."

Her tone caused my anger to surge. "What do you want me to do about it, Pen? I didn't know he was going to ask you, so I'm in shock as much as you are."

She stomped over to stand inches from my face, her bright green eyes boring into mine. "Well, what do you want me to do about it? I thought you'd ask me."

"I don't go to dances, Penny. I haven't since the accident. And why do you care? You've never been one to go all out for that kind of stuff. I thought you'd be okay if we didn't go."

"Well, that's where you're wrong. I never had anyone I wanted to go with until now. You seriously don't want to suck it up and go to a dance with me?" A red color had crept up her neck and into her face, causing her cheeks to nearly match her hair. Her gaze was so intense that I glanced away.

"I've got a lot going on right now. Can we talk about this tomorrow?" I kept my voice soft and even, hoping that would placate her just a bit.

With a shake of her head, she said, "So that's a no from you?"

"We don't need to go to the dance to still be a couple. It's just a dumb high school ritual. I'd rather we just hang out that night."

She nodded, looking like she'd just been slapped. "You're embarrassed of me, aren't you? The great Jake White can't be seen with his so-called girlfriend in public. It's like the only time you want to claim me as your girlfriend is when we're here at home and when no one is watching at school." She turned on her heel, heading for the door with long strides.

I caught her arm just as she opened the door wider than before. "Penny, are you really going to get mad over something ridiculous like this? Why are you so angry?"

When she turned, there were tears in her eyes. "Because I wanted to go with you, Jake. But if you don't want to go, I'll tell Nate yes. Then you and I can do something after."

"You'll tell him yes? Why would you do that?" The stability I usually felt around her seemed to be shifting, and betrayal sliced through me.

"Because I made a promise that I would always give people a chance, even when they've let me down." She glared at me for a few long seconds and said, "It's just a dance, like you said. Let me know if you change your mind before tomorrow."

She pulled her arm from my grasp and disappeared down the stairs. I heard her say something to my mother and then the door open and close, the force of it softer than I'd imagined.

I sat at my desk, unable to concentrate on the book in front of me. Why was she so adamant about going to a dumb dance? And was I being stubborn for not wanting to take her?

Closing my textbook, I changed into some gym shorts and a t-shirt. I fell onto my bed as I tried to work out what I needed to do. We'd agreed we were together. Didn't that merit taking into account my feelings as well? I knew how much girls obsessed over going to formal dances, but I hadn't pictured Penny as being just like them. Why couldn't she understand where I was coming from?

After trudging down the stairs, I opened a cabinet and pulled out a large glass. My mom had bought some whole chocolate milk that day, and I was ready to drown my worries in its rich taste. Sitting at the table, I turned the glass around and around between sips, studying the simple decorations on the outside.

"Jake, are you all right?" my mother's voice called from behind me.

I glanced back and then turned to my milk. "Nothing. Just taking a break from studying."

I heard a few chopping sounds, and soon my mom took the seat next to me, placing a cut apple in front of me. She took a bite of the apple in front of her, and I tried to focus on what I was going to do about the Penny situation.

"You look like you've just had your heart broken, son. Is it Penny?"

Blowing out a breath, I couldn't decide if I wanted to tell her everything. But at this point, talking it out to someone might be better than holding it all in.

"I didn't ask her to prom, and one of my teammates did. She's mad that I won't take her."

My dad's voice from behind startled me. "Plenty of girls in the world, Jake. Believe me. Us Whites don't need to settle down too soon. Don't get serious. Just make this time about you."

"Dave," my mom said, a warning in her voice. It was the first time I'd even seen her look him in the face in months. "Penny is amazing, and look how far Jake has come this year since hanging out with her again. He doesn't need to be as selfish as you."

The fridge opened, and I heard the sound of a can being

opened. I hoped it was the first beer of the night, or I'd have to prepare to be the punching bag once more. But with the conviction in my mother's face, I would gladly protect her. I was usually bitter and angry about my dad's vices, one of which was periodically stepping out on my mother, but his statement caught me off guard. They'd been high school sweethearts, and curiosity burned in me to know if that's the reason he'd started all the troubles in the first place.

It took a few moments for him to answer, and when he looked at me, he said, "I know there are a lot of things I've done that haven't been all that great. I haven't always been the best role model, but I do think being young is a privilege. It's a time when you can figure out who you are, as long as you don't restrict yourself. You have your whole life to settle down and work on a marriage together. Why put yourself through that this early?"

"Penny has always been important to me, Dad. I'm just getting back into her good graces now, and I don't want to screw it up."

"If you don't want to go to the dance, don't go. It's not the end of the world; trust me. Enjoy being a teenager before you have to grow up and be responsible." With that, he walked out of the room and settled in his recliner in front of the TV.

My mother reached her hand over and placed it on top of mine, her words soft. "I think that's something you need to figure out for yourself. And then talk to Penny. If there's anything I've learned over nineteen years of marriage is that without communication, this is what a relationship becomes." She pointed between herself and Dad before standing and rinsing the dishes in the sink.

I twisted my glass again and then picked it up to take a sip. My parents had been high school sweethearts and had married young, from what my grandparents had always said. My mother's sad expression seemed burned into my mind, and I didn't want to end up like my father in ten or twenty years, with an unhappy wife and kids who avoided his angry outbursts. But she'd said that communication would help. I just needed to find a way to work things out with Penny before I hurt her worse than the last time I'd left.

After returning to my room, it was all I could do to pull the covers over me before my eyes closed, bringing back the moments of the accident and the panic I felt every day.

CHAPTER 28

PENNY

I could practically feel the heat coming from my ears, like those old cartoons where fire spews from the sides of their head. Why did Jake have to be so difficult? And why couldn't I be attracted to and like someone with fewer issues? I'd seen him going to dances the year before, seen girls coming to pick him up while watching out my window.

Was it because I didn't get all dolled up every time we went out?

I entered through the front door and I jumped a bit, not realizing I'd shut it so hard.

"What's wrong with you?" Derrick asked, clicking through the channels on the TV.

"Nothing," I said, stomping up the stairs. I didn't feel like rehashing it all with my brother. He'd just tell me I was an idiot for even thinking about a relationship with Jake. He'd seen everything I went through when Mom left, and there had been a number of times when he'd told me to just stay away from Jake.

Maybe he was right.

I slept fitfully that night and then woke up for my morning routine before school.

As the next week passed, I looked back at the past few weeks we'd been "dating," and I realized Jake and I hadn't gone anywhere together. Aside from practices and a few random shifts at the diner, that was the most we were together in public, and he usually waited to kiss me when we were in the privacy of our homes.

It had taken some effort, but I'd successfully avoided Nate for the whole week. I wasn't quite ready to commit to going to prom with him, as my heart was still waiting for Jake to change his mind. I hadn't seen Jake either, though, and even our text messages were short and to the point.

When I finally saw Jake in the hall, my heart rate sped up. Should I pretend not to see him? I felt like I needed some time to formulate my feelings into actual words.

"Hey, Pen," he said, stopping a foot away from me. He stuffed his hands into his pants pockets, his head bowed a bit so it looked like his eyes were hooded.

"Jake."

"I'm sorry about when you came over. I hate this distance between us, but there's just a lot about dances that I can't do." He glanced down at his shoe as he moved it back and forth over the carpet.

"I know. You said it was because of the accident." I kept my tone neutral, hoping he'd be able to share more of the details. I couldn't understand if he didn't explain it.

"I want to take you, but I just…I just can't right now." He glanced up as a few other students walked by and twisted so he was facing the set of lockers against the wall.

As much as I wanted to believe his words, it was his actions that seemed more telling than anything.

The bell rang, causing me to jump and return to the present. If he was going to act like he was embarrassed to be seen with me in public, then we might as well figure this out right now rather than keep wasting time.

"Well, do you still want to date? Or would it be better if we were just friends?" The words felt like rocks coming out of my mouth. I didn't want to just be friends when I knew how much I liked him.

He shrugged and moved the toe of his sneakers across the floor. "It's up to you. If you think a dance is a 'make it or break it' type of thing, maybe friends is the better option."

His whole appearance was more nonchalant than I wanted it to be. Why was he all of a sudden putting up a wall?

"I've got to go. Let me think about it." What else could I say? I wanted to scream and shout for him to stop turning back into the Jake that had inhabited his body ever since we were younger, the one that had disappeared for the last couple of months. But I couldn't do that in the halls, and class might be the better option for me at this point.

I saw him at practice later, more focused than I'd seen him in a long time. He didn't even look up at me as I walked past on my way back to the locker room. My performance at my own practice had been distracted, and Coach Ambrose had noticed.

"What's up, girl? You look like you're going to collapse under the weight of your bat bag." I looked up to see Serena grinning at me.

"What are you doing still at school?" It was the best way to avoid spilling every emotion I'd been feeling all day.

Serena shook her head. "I forgot one of the books I need for an essay due tomorrow. I figured I'd come and get it so I didn't end up failing the class. I'd hate to have to sit out the beginning of volleyball next year because I didn't turn it in."

I chuckled. Serena and I were almost polar opposite when it came to school work, but we both had the same fierce competitive spirit about our sport. "At least you thought that far ahead, right?"

"There's a party tonight near my house. Wanna come?" Serena stepped off the sidewalk, turning to face me.

"I don't know, Serena. I probably shouldn't because of all the AP tests coming up." Oddly, the tone of my voice didn't sound entirely convinced, and my friend picked up on that.

"You'll have the rest of the weekend to study. I might even come join you so I can pass these classes. Just come tonight, and then you can keep me on task for the rest of the weekend."

For some reason, going to a party seemed like a good idea. The one time in my life that it actually did.

I held up my hands. "Yeah, I'll go. It might be nice not to get distracted by my neighbor every five minutes."

Serena glanced behind me in the direction of the ball fields. "Trouble in paradise for the baseball/softball couple?"

"It's just the whole prom thing. He's been acting off the past few days, and I'm not equipped to handle the up-and-down emotions. He's turning back into Jerkface Jake, and I could use a little diversion tonight."

"Perfect! I'll text you the address. Starts at seven, but get there closer to eight." Serena waved goodbye and headed for her little Beetle car. She tore off through the parking lot, nearly hitting a parked car near the exit.

I chuckled and headed inside, dropping my bag in the locker room. Hopefully, I wouldn't regret my decision to go to the party.

* * *

I'D CHOSEN a pair of jean shorts and a t-shirt blouse. I knew the girls were going to give me guff about not dressing up, but if I was going to be uncomfortable somewhere, the least I could do was be comfy with my clothes. I wasn't trying to impress anyone, just trying to figure out what I was going to do with my life. I'd had everything mapped out for the past few years, but having someone to share things with was better than doing it on my own. Trying to meet my mother's expectations even when she wasn't around wasn't the healthiest thing for me.

I found a parking spot somewhat close to the party and made my way to the front door. A note on it said to walk in, so I did, trying to orient myself in the large home. I walked through several of the rooms, searching the faces for one of my friends. I couldn't find any of them and moved out to the backyard.

The view was surprising as the house was built up and able to look out over the small valley. The landscaping was remarkable, with a mini-golf course down toward the fence. It was only about four holes but still impressive.

I rubbed my hands over my upper arms, feeling the chill from the night air. I'd forgotten a jacket once again and turned to head back inside. What was before me caused me to stop in my tracks.

There were several chairs sitting on a little porch to the side of the house, and a bunch of couples were sitting in them. The guy in the second chair over looked familiar, and when the girl sitting on his lap moved to the side, I saw Jake's face, a wide grin covering it.

I took a few steps in their direction, hoping my eyes were just playing tricks on me, when the girl leaned in and kissed him.

A fire erupted in my stomach, and hot tears dripped down my cheeks. He hadn't changed.

I stormed off, pushing through the crowd of people in the main living room and kitchen to the front door. Pulling it closed as hard as I could, I sprinted to my car, not wanting to see anyone else.

Where did you go? I just saw you run through the house. The text was from Serena, and I could barely read it through the tears in my eyes.

Just saw Jake kissing some brunette girl on the deck. I'm going to head home.

I slammed the key into the ignition and took off, pushing the accelerator harder than I'd done in a while. Sure, my car was older and not the best-looking thing in comparison to the other cars students drove, but it had some guts still.

I made the drive in minutes and collapsed on my bed, sobbing, grateful for two days ahead when I didn't have to talk to anyone or do anything. I'd never expected to feel such immense pain. And now I wasn't sure how I would get through another betrayal by Jake White.

CHAPTER 29

JAKE

"You're an idiot!" I heard from behind me. I turned to see Serena, one of Penny's friends with her hands on her hips and looking like she was ready to murder me.

"What are you talking about?" I asked, taking a sip from the Diet Coke in my cup. I raised my eyebrows, waiting for her response.

Serena shoved me in the shoulder and looked like she was trying to keep herself in check. "Why were you kissing some girl outside who wasn't Penny?"

"What do you mean? I didn't kiss anyone. I just got here a few minutes ago. I came with Dax, Nate, and Colt." I motioned in the direction of the kitchen where my two friends were getting a drink. This hadn't been my first choice of places to be, but Dax had insisted we come tonight, saying it would help put things in perspective, whatever that meant. Sure, I'd been a bear the past week, and the only reason I'd agreed to come was to take my mind off the situation with Penny with the loudness of the party, instead of the thoughts overwhelming me in the silence of my room.

Nate walked to my one side, trying to figure out what was going on.

Not the person I wanted to talk to at the moment either. We'd had it out before practice after he'd asked Penny to prom, and I still hadn't said more than a couple of words to him. I'd gone over and over it all in my mind, wondering if I should just cave and go with her to prom, but I didn't want to have a panic attack in front of the whole student body.

An array of emotions played across her face. "You weren't outside on a chair, making out with a brunette girl?"

Now I was getting annoyed. "No. I wouldn't do that. I'm still with Penny. At least, I hope I am."

"You better think fast, then, Jake. Because she was here and took off because she thought she saw you."

My breath caught, and my mind spun with all the scenarios Penny was probably picturing. I'd worked so hard to regain her trust, and although I hadn't been an awesome boyfriend or even friend the past week, I didn't want her to hate me for the rest of my life. Or worse, think that I'd just been gaming her the whole time.

"Did you look out there?" I asked pointing to the back deck.

Serena nodded. "You bet I did. But there was only a weird band couple making out, and there's no way Penny would mistake you for that guy."

"Do you have a car here?" I hoped Serena had a way to get me home. We'd come in Dax's car, and I knew I wasn't going to convince them to leave the party just after we'd arrived.

She nodded. "I can drive you if you want."

"Thank you. Yes, I need to talk to Penny right now." As much as I didn't want to, I turned to Nate. "Tell Dax I've got a ride."

Serena was a surprisingly decent driver, although she preferred speed as we maneuvered through several intersections with ease, making it back to my street in a matter of minutes. She pulled over in front of Penny's house and put the car in park.

"Good luck, Jake. You're going to need it."

"Thanks." I opened the door and stepped out, when she spoke again.

"Fix it. Penny isn't going to survive another heartbreak from you."

Her words caused me to hesitate, and I leaned back down to see her face. "What do you mean 'another heartbreak'?"

"She's liked you since you were kids, or so Kate tells it. You broke her heart the first time you stopped hanging out with her, and I don't think she'll make it through another one. You're the question mark on her notebook."

I felt like the wind had been knocked out of me, and I took a step back. "Uh, thanks." I shut the door and watched as the little compact car moved away. I'd nearly forgotten about the *I heart ?* on her notebook. That was for me?

I turned and ran to her front door, knocking several times and pressing the doorbell over and over again. I'd stop from time to time to listen for any footsteps but just heard a TV coming from the front room.

After at least five minutes, the door swung open fast, causing me to jump back in surprise.

"What do you want, Jake?" Derrick glared at me, and for the first time, Penny's younger brother looked my size.

"I need to talk to Penny. Now. Is she in there?" I stepped up on tiptoe, hoping I'd catch a glimpse of her walking through the room or something.

Derrick shook his head and started closing the door. "I doubt she wants to talk to you right now. She came in sobbing and went straight to her room. Might be a good idea to just leave her alone. You don't want to hurt her worse, do you?"

I shook my head, feeling overwhelming helplessness.

Derrick shut the door with a firm click, and I stepped back, running a hand through my hair. That usually helped me put things in place, but I still had no idea how I was going to get her to listen to me.

Walking around the house to the side, I picked up a few pebbles and tossed them up to Penny's window. There was a dim light on in the room, but even after several minutes, there was no movement I could see.

Sitting in the driveway, I pulled out my phone, opening a text to Penny.

Serena told me what you thought you saw. I got to the party after you left. It wasn't me.

I pressed send, hoping to see a response soon. After another minute, I kept writing.

I wouldn't do that to you, Penny. Please believe me. You mean more to me than anyone ever has. Please call me or text me.

Again I paused, trying to collect my thoughts.

I know I've been a jerk this past week, and I'm sorry.

I sat on the driveway looking up at her window for at least thirty minutes, hoping I'd catch some glimpse of her and be able to signal that I was there.

"Jake, I think it's time to head home," a deep voice called out from the porch at the front. Mr. Davis.

I hung my head and shook it. "She has to know it wasn't me, sir."

Mr. Davis walked over and sat next to me. "Why don't you explain it to me, son?" He put his arm around me, resting his hand on my shoulder.

Emotions ran high, and I wiped my nose with the back of my hand. It took only a few minutes, but I told him every-thing Serena had told me and how I'd come back here as soon as I'd heard.

He nodded a few times, looking like he was chewing on

something as he studied the ground in front of us. "Well, Jake, just know that things will work out. But that's not to say you should just wait for her to call you. You're going to have to prove, in some way, that it wasn't you at the party. You know how Penelope gets with things. Once something is in her mind, it's hard to pry her from that opinion." He paused and looked over at me, studying my face. "You're worth it, and she's so much happier when she's with you."

"You don't think we're too young to be dating?" My parents' words had popped up in my head, suddenly making me doubt everything I'd been worried about over the past half hour.

Mr. Davis chuckled. "Not a bit. I met my wife in high school, and we started dating a few weeks later. We went through a lot in those first few years and then again once we got married. But I wouldn't change it for the world, even knowing how things would turn out between us. She gave me two of the greatest gifts ever, and I'm grateful for that."

"You didn't regret it when she left?" I winced, wishing I could've softened the blow a little bit.

A sad smile took over, and he said, "Nope. Well, maybe the first few days, but there are things I never could've given her, and if she felt she needed those things above her family, I wasn't going to stand in her way. As long as I have those kids under my roof to love, I will forever be grateful for that."

We sat in silence for several moments as I tossed around the ideas he'd given me. It was a completely different outlook to the one my father had offered up the week before. As if sensing my hesitation, he spoke again.

"You two have been through more in the past five years than most adults, and even though you had a falling out for a while, I think you're both stronger for it. You know how much you need the other one. Just keep moving forward, Jake. She'll come around."

"Thank you, sir." My voice came out gruff, but I felt the words resonate with me. Penny was the person in life I couldn't lose. It had just taken way longer than it should have for me to realize that.

He patted my back. "Get some sleep. You're going to need it to come up with a plan to win her back."

I waved good night and headed to my house, glancing up at the window in the hopes that I'd at least see her silhouette.

More determined than before, I had to come up with a plan to convince her how much I really did care.

CHAPTER 30

PENNY

I woke up feeling like I'd been hit by a train, every muscle sore from an awkward night of sleep. I'd had so many dreams about what had happened the night before, and I wanted to just forget about it and move on, go back to the goals I'd set at the beginning of the year.

Checking my phone, I realized I had a shift at the diner I'd forgotten about, meaning I had to hurry or I'd be late.

After throwing on my uniform, I ran out the door, trying to pull my hair into a ponytail. I turned the key in the ignition and heard the one sound I didn't want to hear when I was in a hurry. The *click-click* of the engine as it wouldn't start. I tried it again, using every trick I could think of to get it working.

A tap came at the window, and I jumped, hitting my elbow on the console next to me. The awful feeling of hitting a nerve rippled through my forearm, and I bit my tongue to keep from shouting out.

"What do you want?" I asked Jake after rolling down the window a crack.

"I'm heading to the diner. I can take you if you want."

Shaking my head, I said, "I'd rather eat dirt." I sounded just like when we'd started talking more, and part of me was sorry our relationship had turned back to this.

"Penny, it wasn't me at the party last night. I promise. You can ask Dax and Colt. You have to believe me. Did you get my texts last night? I tried to explain—"

"I deleted them, and I don't have to believe anything," I said, leaning forward to try the ignition again. It made the same sound, and I dropped my head to the steering wheel. Why couldn't it just work when I needed it to?

"What if I don't talk the entire way to the diner? Will you let me give you a ride?"

I lifted my head but avoided looking at him. Unbuckling my seatbelt, I opened the door. "Not a peep," I said, pointing a finger at him.

The drive over was awkward, but at that point, I was too hurt to care about it. I'd deleted his number sometime during the night, and the text messages that had come in went into the trash as well. Reading them would have brought more tears, and I'd spilled more in one night than I had in a long time. My wounds felt raw already without his excuses, like they'd been clawed out by a vicious animal.

Once he parked the Jeep, I jumped out, running in to make it only a minute or two late. Jake was right behind me, grabbing an apron from the rack just after I had.

"You have to understand I wouldn't do that to you, Penny. I know you asked for time to think it over, and I've been a jerk. I'm so sorry—"

"That's enough!" I raised my hands, trying to catch my breath before I spoke again. "Just leave me alone for now, please. I need to get to work." I didn't even acknowledge Lou, walking out onto the dining floor, trying to regain some semblance of calm.

Seeing Claudia, I walked over to her. "Where do you need me?"

"Thank goodness you made it. I was beginning to think this would be the shift that killed me in the end." She directed me to my assigned booths, and I got to work, making sure to focus on the customer's words, even if my mind drifted every few seconds to the boy carrying a gray bin and a washcloth.

Each time I saw him, the image of him kissing a girl popped up, squashing any emotion I felt for him. I was just another dumb girl who'd fallen for his charms.

As much as I wanted to believe he was telling the truth, I needed to move on. To make it through my junior year and then get some kind of scholarship. Anything to get me away from this town and Jake White.

CHAPTER 31

JAKE

I'd never felt more miserable than I did over the next few days. I wracked my brain, trying to think of some way to prove to Penny that it wasn't me at the party kissing some other girl. I hadn't kissed anyone but her in months, and I wasn't planning on kissing anyone else. Ever. None of the other girls I'd kissed had made me feel the way she did.

"Who rained on your parade?" Dax asked, slamming me in the shoulder with his own.

We were in the locker room, getting ready for an away game, and I wasn't in the mood for anything but sleep. It was going to be a long night if something didn't change.

"I still don't know how to tell Penny I wasn't the one making out with another girl at that party last weekend. She thought she saw me. Do I have any doppelgangers that go to this school?" It sounded weird to think about it like that, more conceited than actually helpful, but I didn't know another way to phrase it.

"Not that I know of," Dax said, pulling off his t-shirt and throwing it onto the growing pile of clothes in his locker. He turned to Ben and asked, "Is there a guy who looks like White at the school?"

Ben shook his head, shrugging. "None that I know of. But maybe in the sophomore or freshman class? I don't know many of them since most of my classes consist of juniors and seniors."

Colt spoke up. "I might know of someone. Let me check, and I'll let you know." The tone of his voice gave me an odd sense of hope, even if it was only a sliver. If the kid looked like me, I wasn't sure how I'd be able to convince Penny he was the one at the party except by dragging him over to her at some point and explaining the whole thing. But I'd just have to wait and see if Colt was even able to locate someone semi-close to my appearance.

We won the away game, and I even made a few great plays despite my brain not being completely focused with every pitch.

Even with the win, Coach Maddox was brutal in practice the next day, keeping us over three hours in what had turned into unbearable heat. I'd been through some rough practices, but this one seemed to top them all. And he kept yelling out my name, making sure I knew he was watching. When it was finally time to head home, I walked back to my Jeep, feeling like my feet had turned to cement.

Up ahead, I saw a dark-haired girl who looked somewhat familiar. She turned and smiled at me, waving a bit. Great, she was probably someone I'd made out with at some point, and now I couldn't remember her name. Several other students milled around behind her, a few I recognized. It must have been one of the groups working off tardies. Something I still needed to do.

I nodded and averted my eyes, hoping she wouldn't try talking to me. A nice convertible pulled up with the top down and a guy with dark brown hair in the driver's seat.

"Hey, Jake. That guy could probably pass as you." Dax slapped my back, his loud words drawing the attention of the driver.

Colt came up next to me, out of breath. "Hey, I saw that guy at the party. He's the one I was thinking of yesterday."

Without thinking, I walked over to the car and asked, "Were you at a party this last weekend? Down by Chester Street?"

The guy gave me a look like I'd lost all my marbles but nodded. "Yeah, I was at a party this weekend. That's where I met this bombshell." He motioned to the girl, who opened the door and slid into the passenger seat. She leaned forward, and he met her with a kiss to the lips, lingering longer than made even me feel comfortable.

"You didn't happen to be sitting out on the patio when you met, did you?" It was a long shot, but I might as well give it a try.

The girl looked at me, biting her bottom lip with her eyebrows drawn together as if I was going to reveal I was some cop and she was under arrest. "How would you know that?"

Breathing a sigh of relief, I said, "So, it was you? Yes?" I raised my thumbs like I'd officially lost it.

"What of it, man?"

"I just need to know. My girlfriend thought she saw me making out with a brunette at the party, but I wasn't there at the same time she was. I just need to prove it wasn't me."

The guy grinned like he knew exactly how I was feeling. "Yeah, that was us. A few people dubbed that the make-out deck. Sounds like a fitting spot for our first hangout, don't you think, Shari?"

She giggled, and I groaned, wondering how many times I'd done something just like that. Even knowing her name didn't ring a bell.

"What's your name? I haven't seen you around here before," Dax asked the guy, bringing me back to the goal of this encounter.

"Carl Sumner. I'm a senior over at Tristan Prep. A few of my friends wanted to crash the party, and it turned out to be a great night for me."

"Can I get your number?" I asked.

When the guy gave me a weird look, I shook my head. "It's not like that, man. I just need some way to prove to Penny that I didn't cheat on her. When I think of something, I'd call you to help me out. Is that all right?"

"Sure, man. I got you." He took my phone and typed out his number, giving it back to me after. "Good luck."

He waved, and they took off, leaving tire marks next to the curb where he'd peeled out.

"What are the odds you'd see that guy right now? The stars must be aligning to make your life just a little bit easier." Dax slapped my back with his open palm, and I focused on controlling the pain rather than grimacing.

"That's just half of the battle. The other is convincing Penny I'm not a cheater. Well, anymore." The momentary bit of hope I'd felt as all the pieces of the puzzle fell into place was replaced by every other emotion to dampen it.

The end of the year was coming, and I needed her to cheer me on and reassure me I could be the person she'd believed I could be. The sooner the better.

CHAPTER 32

"You look stunning!" Kate clapped her hands together after applying some colored lip balm to my lips. We'd planned to get ready for prom together at her house, and I was glad we had. It kept me from fuming every time I looked out the window toward Jake's house.

Looking in the mirror, I smiled, the first genuine smile in, well, at least two weeks, ever since my confrontation with Jake at his house. She'd curled my hair in soft beachy waves and had done my makeup in a simple, more elegant fashion than the last time I'd let my friends dress me up. The dress she'd helped me find at the thrift store could not have fit better if it had been tailored just for me. The silver beaded bodice and tulle made me feel like a princess. And I didn't want to cry when I'd looked at the price tag.

As I stared at my reflection, I saw the reason I'd wanted this night to happen so badly. My mother's prom pictures were always over the top, but she'd somehow managed to make it work with the big hair and crazy styles. I didn't have that type of fashion sense, but I wanted one night where I wasn't the softball player or the tomboy.

If only it was with the person I wanted to be with and not one of his baseball buddies.

"Have you heard from Jake lately?" Kate asked, as if sensing my mood had changed.

I shook my head. "He stopped calling and texting two days ago. I don't know whether to be sad or relieved, to be honest."

"Well, it might help if you let him tell his side of the story. Maybe there was a reason he was—"

"Like a bottom-dwelling fish sucking up all the scum on the bottom of the tank?" My voice was flat, but Kate's eyes went wide.

She pursed her lips and shook her head. "Someone's trying to compare her boyfriend to things she's studying in class. Probably not a good thing."

"Ex-boyfriend," I corrected.

"You might want to tell him that. It might help you get over him faster."

The doorbell rang, and we hurried to gather up our things, slipping on shoes and grabbing clutches. I felt a bit nervous as I barely knew Nate, but I was determined to make the most of the night. To add it to the small list of high school memories I wanted to keep.

Kate had been asked by one of the student body officers, but since he was part of the group we were going with for the dance, that meant I would at least have a friend close throughout the whole thing.

"Wow, you look amazing," Nate said when I met him at the door. He was dressed in a black suit, his hair done. He was a cute guy, but I kept going back to thoughts of what Jake would look like dressed up in something more formal.

Shaking off the thought, I stepped back to let them inside and smiled. "Thank you. You clean up pretty well yourself."

After the traditional exchange of corsage and boutonniere, and Kate's mother taking a million and one pictures of us in different poses, we finally walked outside.

"A limo?" Kate asked, jumping up and down as much as her high, high heels allowed.

A small pit formed in my stomach, and guilt flooded me. I wasn't interested in Nate like this, and I could only hope he hadn't gone over the top because he had feelings for me.

"You didn't have to do this, Nate," I mumbled so only he could hear me. I slid into the long car and smiled slightly at two couples on the other bench.

Nate put his arm on the back of the seat and leaned in, his lips close to my ear. "I promise this wasn't my idea. I'm not really into the big showy kind of stuff. Are you uncomfortable?"

I licked my lips, trying to figure out how to word it. "I just don't want you to get the wrong idea. I'm excited about tonight and all, but I barely know you."

He chuckled, and something about it put me at ease. "No worries. I've always thought you were a cool girl. I just thought you'd be someone fun to take to a dance."

Feeling like an idiot, I smiled and nodded, trying to focus on everything but his face. I needed to keep that in mind. Just have fun, be myself, and then go back to being the nerdy softball player by Monday.

We ate dinner at someone's indoor basketball court, complete with waiters and candlelight. After we'd eaten the main course, I leaned over to Nate and said, "Who planned this?"

Nate pointed out the guy who'd asked Kate to the dance. "He's got a big thing for your friend. I think he was hoping that by going all out, she'd notice him or even start dating him."

"None of your baseball friends decided to go to the dance?" I asked, taking a small bite from the cheesecake that had appeared before me. It was smooth and velvety, nearly melting on my tongue.

"Dax and Ben did. But since I'm a sophomore, I've got different friends outside of baseball and I decided to go with them. Hopefully that's okay with you?"

I nodded, somewhat surprised to find he was a year younger. He meshed so well with the other juniors that I'd just assumed he was one. "I'm good. Enjoying this cheese-cake. This will definitely be a night to remember."

We chatted back and forth until the group stood to leave, and I found we had a lot more in common than I'd originally thought. I didn't feel anything crazy when he touched me or put his hand on my back to guide me, but at least he wasn't a creeper.

We all piled back into the limo and drove through the streets of town to the large city building where the dance was being held. Nate helped me out of the car and hooked his arm next to him so I could put my hand through it as he guided me into the building.

"Wow, Kate. You guys did a great job with the decora-tions," I said, talking loud enough that she could hear me a few steps in front.

"We weren't in charge of the decorations on this one, but the committee did do a great job, didn't they?" She smiled and turned to glance around.

I took in the strings of white lights and tulle, the elegant flower decorations on several tables, and the beautiful marble that made up the floor.

We walked over to the dance floor, and Nate asked, "Would you like to dance?"

I nodded and wrapped my arms around his neck, making sure there was room between us as we swayed along to the slower song.

As the tune came to an end, I felt a tap on my shoulder and turned to find a guy I'd never met standing next to me. His hair was dark, and he had a similar build to Jake, but I shook off that thought as quickly as it came.

"Yes?" I asked, curious as to what he could want.

A girl I recognized as Shari Donovan came and stood next to him, leaning her head on his shoulder and giving me a dreamy smile.

"I've been told that you mistook me and my girlfriend for someone else at the party last weekend. We were kissing in one of the chairs on the deck."

I squinted, calling up a mental picture of that night. It had been dark, with the soft lights behind them backlighting their faces. But I'd been so sure it was Jake.

"You were in the second chair over?" The words seemed to loosen something within me, and I had to choke back a sob.

"Yep. That was us. We were there for quite a while."

I nodded. "Uh, th-thank you for telling me that."

The couple walked away, him practically carrying her as she held on to his side.

Nate's hand touched my arm. "Are you okay?"

I held back the tears as much as I could, hoping to not break down in front of him. Kate would kill me if I ruined her makeup job before we'd even been there fifteen minutes.

"I'm sorry. I just need some air. I'll be right back." I walked in the direction of some large glass doors, feeling the breeze even before I made it there. I pulled the air in as though I'd been without oxygen for minutes, drinking it in as I stared up at the stars above.

"You look beautiful," a voice said from behind me.

I froze, not wanting to believe it could be the person I wanted it to be. I didn't move for several seconds, and then I saw him move into my peripheral, leaning on the small railing of the balcony. He was wearing a dark blue suit with a striped silver tie, and just one look at him made my knees go weak. I turned my gaze forward, hoping to steel myself against whatever he was going to say.

I glanced at him and back to the stars, unsure of what to say. "I thought you didn't do dances." I wiped away a tear as gingerly as possible, dabbing right under the eye with my finger.

"I swore I wouldn't go to another dance after...well, after the accident. It brought back too many memories and guilt. But I knew that if I was going to break that promise to myself, I wanted it to be with you." He looked up at me with hooded eyes, probably worried about how I would react. "I know I've been a jerk, Penny, but I want you to know I love you. I think I've always loved you. And after you went through all the crap with your mom, I didn't want to hurt you."

"How would you have hurt me worse at thirteen than you did?" I turned so I was leaning against the railing but looking directly at him. As much as my mind wanted to dwell on the three little words, I had to resolve all the other doubts before he shut down or shut me out.

His jaw twitched, and I could detect sadness from the side of his face I could actually see. But when he turned to look at me, the chocolate-brown of his eyes pulled me in, just like they always did.

"That was the failed logic of a thirteen-year-old, Penny. I thought I was going to turn out just like my father, and I didn't want you to be part of the destruction. And then he talked to me two weeks ago after you told me you wanted to go to this dance, giving me this story about how it would never work out if we started our relationship in high school. I'm sorry for being so weird and standoffish. I knew how much it had taken you to trust me, and I didn't want to break that trust again."

I allowed his words to sink in. I could only imagine what he'd gone through after getting advice from his father. "You actually listened to your father when it came to relationships?"

"It was both my parents. They were high school sweethearts, and look where they ended up. But I talked to your dad, and he said he and your mom had been together in high school as well."

"Sounds like the track records for high school sweethearts are slim to none." I tried to keep the emotion from my voice, but I had to turn, looking out on the view of the city.

Jake's fingers lightly touched my arm, sending little shots of electricity pulsing through my skin. "What your dad said hit me, though. He said he wouldn't change anything, even if he'd known how things would end up, because he had you and Derrick. The thing that stuck with me from my mom was that communication was key. Penny, there are plenty of people who make it forever after dating in high school. I love you enough to be one of those couples."

Goosebumps popped up on my skin as I concentrated on his words. "You love me?"

He nodded, giving me a hesitant smile as he closed the distance between us. "I do, Penelope Davis. I'm probably not the guy of your dreams, but I'm head over heels for you. You make me want to be a better person and have a vision for the future."

I bit my lip, hoping the tears would stay tucked inside rather than spilling out everywhere. "I'm pretty sure I love you too, Jake White."

He leaned forward, matching his lips to mine, and I felt the electricity I'd been missing over the past two weeks.

When we broke apart, I jumped. "I should probably go. I'm here with Nate." As much as I didn't want to leave, I didn't want my date to feel bad about me ditching him.

Jake shook his head. "No worries. I already talked to him. And I think he might have found someone to talk to." He pointed to the dance floor where Nate swayed to a slow song with a girl at least eight inches shorter than he was. The girl looked somewhat familiar, but I couldn't place her.

"Well, that's probably a good thing. Nate reminds me a lot of a more athletic version of my brother." I chuckled, and Jake laughed, the sound healing the wounds I'd been feeling.

"That's just one of the things I love about you, Penny. You always know how to make me laugh." He held out his hand and did a little bow. "May I have this dance?" he asked in an awful British accent.

I put my hand in his. "Yes, you may, as long as you never talk like that again."

He led me out onto the dancefloor where he pulled me close and swayed to the soft music. Leaning in, he whispered in my ear, "Did I surprise you by coming tonight?"

"I'm definitely shocked that you came, but then again, you're known for the perfect play in baseball. Now you can say you know how to do it to win back your girlfriend." I grinned at him, and he kissed me again, his lips soft. I knew this night was going to be one to remember.

EPILOGUE

Penny

The summer passed quickly with tournaments for the two of us all over Texas and a few other states in the South. Jake finished his indentured service at the diner and got a job at the local dealership, washing and cleaning out cars when they came in. It was tough work, but he enjoyed it more than bussing tables. His mother served his father with divorce papers, and while Mr. White hadn't made it easy at first, things were progressing, and Mrs. White was going to be able to keep the house until all the kids graduated.

We'd entered the fall of our senior year, and mail had started piling up from different colleges around the country. With each envelope opened, I would study the material, making sure I had all the facts before making one of the biggest decisions of my life.

Jake and I were watching a movie in our family room when a call came through on my cell phone.

"Is this Penelope Davis?"

"Yes," I said, a bit hesitant.

"This is Michelle Andrews, head softball coach at the University of Texas. I've seen you play several times throughout the past summer, and I'm impressed. I'd like to offer you a full-ride scholarship to pitch for us."

My mouth dropped open, and I squeezed Jake's forearm, my eyes wide with excitement. "That sounds amazing." I racked my brain, trying to figure out what to say to that. The University of Texas had been high on my list for a while, but a full-ride scholarship? I was tongue-tied.

Jake took the phone from me and spoke into it. "Thank you for the offer. She'll call you back in a bit." He hung up and stared at me. "So? What was that about?"

"University of Texas." I paused, my brain still processing the words from the coach. "Full-ride scholarship."

"No way! That's amazing. And their program is awesome. You should commit to them." He wrapped me in his strong arms, and I'd never been happier.

When I pulled back, I looked at him, feeling a twist in my stomach. "But what about you? Weren't you thinking about Odessa or one of the schools in Western Texas? I don't want to be that far away from you."

He got a goofy grin and said, "I just got an email from Wharton earlier today, and they want me to play there. They have a bunch of pro scouts who are alumni from there, and Coach Maddox thinks that would be a great place to start. We'd only be an hour away from each other, and we could drive to see one another on weekends or whatever we have free."

"Are you serious? I've been worrying about it for the last few months, wondering how we would be close enough to see each other while still in school. Because I don't think I could make it to the breaks before seeing you." I leaned forward and gave him a peck on the lips, feeling the adrenaline rush through me.

"It might still be hard with practices and games, but we'll find a way to make it work."

We settled back to watch the movie, my brain abuzz with excitement. It was something we'd both been working hard for, the chance to pursue our futures, and all the hard work had paid off. People said the odds were against us, having started dating so young, but I was ready for the future, ready to cheer on my shortstop and see where his talents led him.

And I was ready to chase my dream of becoming a family therapist. It would be a lot of work and several years, but we'd get through it. Life wasn't a perfect game, but there were moments that were perfect, and I couldn't ask for anything better.

Thank you for reading *The Perfect Play!* If you enjoyed it, I would love to see a review from you. You can also subscribe to Britney's newsletter by visiting britneymmills.com